STO

BORU

The Story of an Irish Wolfhound

IN COMMON WITH ALL IRISH WOLFHOUNDS, BORU WAS A ONE-MAN DOG. HE LIVED WITHIN HIMSELF, SCORNING TO FAWN FOR FAVOURS

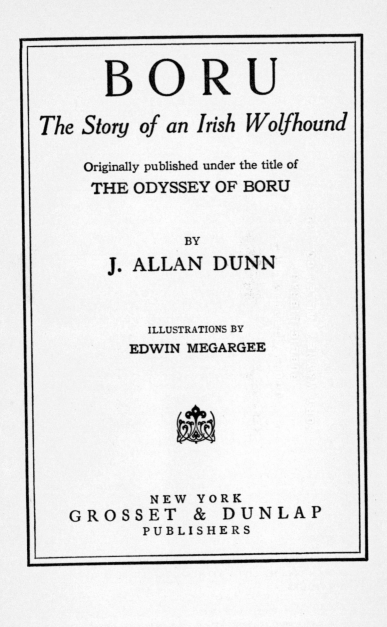

BORU

The Story of an Irish Wolfhound

Originally published under the title of
THE ODYSSEY OF BORU

BY

J. ALLAN DUNN

ILLUSTRATIONS BY
EDWIN MEGARGEE

NEW YORK
GROSSET & DUNLAP
PUBLISHERS

To
JOHN MORGAN LEWIS

INTRODUCTION

Writing acceptable fiction on technical subjects undoubtedly is the most difficult of all forms of creative writing. Those who know the subject are always prone to be supercritical. And of all subjects that form the backbone of fiction, not another possesses more technical minds anxious to criticize and to be amused than the dog.

That is the reason why it is so difficult to write an acceptable dog story. There are too many critical readers. It is not surprising, therefore, that, while an author may know dogs—and he must know dogs to be able to write dog fiction—he often puts into his stories such astonishing statements that other technical dog minds think they are absurd.

But they are not absurd. All who own dogs know, that dogs do such astonishing things that the exploitations of these incidents seem only the fancies of a creative brain.

To my mind, J. Allan Dunn is one of the few writers able to create a dog character in a way that is acceptable both to those who know and to those who do not know dogs. Although there is sentiment in his dog stories, the heart beats are always subservient to the character study. Dunn's dogs are real dogs. They are just the type that you like and I like—dogs that, no doubt, have actually lived prior to appearing between the covers of a book.

Take Boru as an example. There is no questioning the fact that Boru is a real dog—an Irish wolfhound that only could have been created by one who knows the breed. He is a study of canine psychology that is almost unequaled in the world of fiction. Descended from a line of colorful dog kings, Boru carried under his shaggy coat a being just as elemental, just as romantic, as that of any human out of the legends of Erin's Isle.

In Boru there has been exemplified all the undying devotion, the quick-kindling temper and spontaneity of purpose which is connected with the race whose firesides his ancestors guarded.

To me, as a lover of dogs, there is nothing quite like the Odyssey of this big Irish wolfhound. His wanderings have taken me out into the open, and there I have seen a great primitive love. I rejoiced in Boru's freedom; I was happy when he was glad; and I am not ashamed to say that I dropped a tear when Boru lost his mate—the white she-wolf of the hills.

All this I did, because Boru is a real dog, created by a

man who knows and loves dogs. And created, perhaps, more for the entertainment of his dog-loving friends, than for the amusement of a less discriminating public.

J. E. de Mund

President, American Kennel Club

CONTENTS

ILLUSTRATIONS

BORU

The Story of an Irish Wolfhound

CHAPTER ONE

HERITAGE

Boru basked in the sun, stretched out luxuriantly asleep, his great bulk covered with coarse, crisply curling gray hair.

Dempsey, once billed as the "Lion King," before a bad mauling destroyed his nerve and left him glad of his job as keeper of the little menagerie of Bilton's Imperial Circus, looked admiringly at the big Irish wolfhound. While he watched, Boru's jaws snapped together with a vicious click of the gleaming teeth, and his legs worked spasmodically as he whined in his dreams.

Dempsey, as usual, was a little the worse—though he would have styled it a little better—for liquor.

"I wonder," he said whimsically; "troth, I wonder now what ye think ye're chasin' after in your sleep? A cat likely. I misdoubt if ye ever saw a rabbit in your life, let alone bigger game. 'Tis a mortal shame for the likes of ye, with your forbears trained, mebbe, by Brian Boru himself, to be goin' through tricks in a circus like a skin-shaved poodle. 'Tis wolves ye should be dreamin' of. Would

1

ye know one if ye saw it, I wonder? Faith, I've a mind
to introduce ye, an' see what ye think of them."

He whistled to the slumbering dog. Boru stirred and
opened great luminous eyes at the ex-trainer. The brown
iris was so dark it seemed to blend into the velvety
black pupil. He yawned, stood at the top of his height,
full three feet at the shoulders, bowed his muzzle between
his outstretched forelegs, yawned again, raised his head,
and regarded Dempsey with grave scrutiny.

Boru was not demonstrative nor overkeen at the over-
tures of strangers. Moreover, he was tired and bored
from a long trip in cramped quarters and the morning's
rehearsal. But something in him responded to the light
in Dempsey's blue-gray eyes, and, sensing a bond of understanding, he wagged his tail in token of amity.

The keeper's hand dropped confidently to the big grizzly
head, scratched behind the ears, passed over the powerful
shoulders, and patted the arching ribs. Boru thrust his
muzzle against the man's sleeve in return for the caress,
and Dempsey unfastened the leash chain from the wagon
wheel to which it was shackled.

"Come on," he said; "an' I'll introduce ye to the Countess Vladoska's troupe of untamed Siberian wolves."

Boru followed amicably to where the traveling wagons
of the menagerie were ranged. A puff of wind brought

the musky odor of the beasts to his nostrils, and he halted, the hair lifting about his neck and along his spine.

It was the same hostile scent that had disturbed his recent slumbers and kept him awake most of the night before, with vague stirrings of something familiar, though not to be linked up with definite memory.

A growl rumbled deep in his throat. Dempsey patted his head reassuringly.

" 'Tis the true McDermot breed ye are," he said. "Come on!"

Boru, every faculty alert, conscious of hostility close at hand, watchful of a possible surprise, moved on springy tiptoes to the wagons. At the grating cough of a puma, impatient for mealtime, his lips lifted and the swift saliva overflowed his gums.

As they entered the lane between the cages, the far-away undefined remembrance strove once more to assert itself as Boru, with Dempsey holding him short-leashed, passed the mangy bears, the ancient lion, and the cage-born pumas that pressed close to their bars to watch the intruder.

They came to a halt in front of a cage where a dog wolf and his mate had stopped pacing their narrow quarters and stood with ruffed fur, their fangs agrin and greenish-yellow eyes flaming.

The dog wolf gave a sudden snarl, and Boru whirled in his tracks to face him, tugging at his chain.

"Mr. Boru, Wolfhound, from Ireland," said Dempsey. "Make you acquainted with Mr. and Mrs. Wolf, said to be from Siberia, though Montana would hit the mark closer, I'm thinkin'. Two more in the next cage."

Boru glared at the wolves with eager, implacable hatred. The uneasy stir within him was a puzzle no longer. Centuries slid away as hereditary training asserted itself, and the inbred instinct of his race, the spirit of his fathers, engendered when they ran in the wolf packs of the war-loving, sport-craving Irish kings, mounted. Here were his ancient enemies, his natural foes. The slaver dripped from his red tongue, his eyes blazed, his jaws ached with the desire to tear and slash and rend. He had come suddenly into his heritage of hate.

"Ye'd like to get at 'em, wouldn't ye, ye big Irish divvle? It's spoilin' for a scrap ye are. Steady, boy!"

The rumbling growl in Boru's throat turned to a hot bark of fury as he lunged forward, straining against the leash, rearing high, his hundred and thirty pounds nearly overpowering the big Irishman.

The wolves echoed his threat, crouching low, their muzzles thrust between the lowest bar and the floor of the cage. The two in the adjoining compartment repeated the fighting cry. In the instant every beast in the menagerie had taken up the challenge with snarl and cough and roar of defiance against their sworn enemy, the Dog, outlaw of the wild, deserter of the clan, ally of Man the Conqueror. The primeval hatred flared until the place was a pandemonium of brutish enmity.

"Come away with ye!" cried Dempsey, tugging at Boru with both hands set in his collar, scarlet and breathless with the exertion of restraining the furious hound.

Boru, his forefeet off the ground, struggling, half choked by Dempsey, sounded his deep-chested roar, his eyes crimson with fighting lust, every muscle set for action, every sinew and tendon tautened to steel springs.

Struggling hard to reach the bars and come to close quarters with the evil-eyed wolf and his consort, who mocked his wild desire to combat with their red tongues and gleaming tusks; his spirit, ignoring odds, leaped to the challenge. But he did not dispute the supremacy of Dempsey. He had known man too long and too closely, kennel-bred and trained as he was, to resent the authority he had respected from puppyhood.

"You're game, all right," panted Dempsey, braced hard to offset Boru's frantic plungings; "but ye've raised seventeen kinds of a ruction. Here comes my boss an' yours

—an' trouble walkin' arm in arm betwixt the two of 'em, ready for action."

Bilton, of Bilton's Imperial Circus and Matchless Menagerie of Man-eaters, waddled as swiftly as his fat permitted to the cause of the turmoil, his empurpled, three-chinned countenance, inflamed as much by indulgence as by exposure, working angrily.   Another man was with him, tall and thin, with spiky, dyed mustaches and imperial blackly emphasizing the scowl upon his sallow face.

"What's all this racket about?" demanded Bilton wheezily.

The tall man came forward and added his strength to subdue Boru's rearing plunges, setting his fingers into the dog's collar and pressing in his knuckles, shutting off Boru's breathing.

"What in blazes you tryin' ter do, gittin' a dog all worked up like that, an' them raisin' Cain at the rehearsal as it is?"

"I was but by way of givin' the dog a trifle of divarsion, Mister Holdini," Dempsey answered.   "Steady there, won't ye?"

Boru was beside himself with desire to answer the taunts that came from the cages.   The throaty clamor of the beasts conveyed the deadliest insult of their species, couched in a universal language that he thoroughly understood.

The blood surged to his brain, and he lunged desperately forward, dragging the two men, stumbling, behind him. The fury of his leap carried him nearly to the bars of the cage, and his jaws snapped just short of the grating. He caught fetid breath from the red gullets of the wolves as they retreated from his rush and he fought to get free, rearing high between the two men.

"Lend a hand here, Bilton, can't ye?" called Holdini. "The dog's crazy."

Bilton threw his heavy weight into the balance, and Boru, half choked, subdued by main force, was dragged reluctantly away.

He kept his head twisted back toward the cages as they hauled him protestingly along; indignant, sounding deep notes of defiance. To retreat was contrary to every suddenly aroused element of his new-found self. Always under the watchful eye of a trainer as a valuable asset of Holdini's Canine Circus, he had yet to achieve his first fight. He knew nothing of cowardice or bravery as applied to himself but, in the light of awakened intuition, he sensed that retreat meant a handicap for future conflicts.

He went out between Dempsey and Holdini with his legs braced, his spine rigid, his tail whipping stiffly, trying to appear indifferent to the derisive cries of the beasts crowding to the bars to watch his enforced retreat.

One thought formed itself and remained paramount—to settle accounts some day with the wolves—the others might go—but, some time, he would meet the wolf dog and his mate who had mocked him, and their mates in the next cage for that matter, come one, come all, strength for strength, fang for fang, and decide the mastery.

The two men led him away to the main tent, and Dempsey came back, wiping his sweaty forehead, to Bilton, who had stayed in the menagerie.

"You're drunk again, Dempsey. You go put your head in a bucket, then get 'em quieted down. Next time you get teed up you lose your job. That goes."

Dempsey stuck his tongue in his cheek as Bilton waddled off.

"I'd not be losing much, at that," he muttered. "But that's sure some dog! 'Tis a shame to make a trick mutt out of him."

He took a dingy flask from his pocket and surveyed the dubious contents with anticipatory appreciation.

"A man," he said, "is usually only forty per cent human, an' damn few of them is thoro'breds. But a dog is generally all dog, and Boru—bless the Irish name of him—is a hundred and one per cent. Here's to him!"

Bilton's Circus was imperial in name only. It was a two-ring, no-elephant affair that left the cities to bigger enterprises and played the Lumber Circuit, taking in towns and concentration camps of the logging industry, where it was a recognized and welcome institution.

It had just come out of winter quarters for the first pitch of the season at Tamarack. Holdini's Canine Circus was an added attraction. When Holdini—whose real name was Green—won over by the persuasive, if husky, eloquence of Bilton, decided to invest the saving of years of successful vaudeville in Bilton's Imperial Circus and Mammoth Menagerie of Matchless Man-eaters, he took his act with him, thereby placing himself on the salary list as well as becoming a partner in the profits so rosily pictured to him. He and his dogs had arrived the night before, and he had spent the morning in arduous rehearsal, trying to accustom the dogs to their new surroundings, changing the act to better suit the big ring.

In the afternoon he went at it again. The dogs, used to the narrower space of the theater stage, made mistakes despite their efforts to understand, and Holdini worked until his temper was in rags and his performers in tired rebellion.

Boru went through his part tolerantly. In common with all wolf-hounds, he was a one-man dog, and, as far as the rest of the troupe was concerned, indifferent to them. He lived within himself, scorning to fawn for favors like his fellows. For Holdini, whose smiling stage deportment gave small hint of his harsher methods of control in private, he had little liking.

The performance itself, excitedly enjoyed by most of the dogs, he despised, aside from the leaping. Then he loved the strong thrust of his hocks, the spring of his muscles, the surge over the obstacle, secretly enjoyed the applause that fell to his share.

At the end of the afternoon, two great Danes that, with Boru, took a prominent part in the final tableau of the act, failed twice to understand the command, and Holdini, losing his self-control, slashed indiscriminately with his whip. The lash writhed across Boru's muzzle, stinging like a red-hot wire, and he wrinkled back his upper lip, snarling in threatening resentment.

Holdini, realizing his own condition, dodged the issue, cursing Dempsey under his breath for Boru's attitude; but, in his anxiety for a smooth first performance that evening, willing to avoid trouble.

It was not good judgment on Holdini's part. Boru had seen the great Danes rebel before and be whipped until they cringed. So far he had been too bored with his tricks to show active rancor. In a dim way, he had felt that his service paid for what he received in the way of food and shelter, an innate idea which ran back to the time when the first of his kind came into camp and served as guardian in return for the warmth of the fire and the remnant of the kill. But he would not have suffered punishment unjustly or have tolerated it at all beyond his sense of values, and the submissive great Danes had gone down in his estimation accordingly, as now his own allegiance to Holdini slipped in the clutch.

Rehearsal over at last, Holdini fed his troupe and picketed them outside the main tent to rest until dark.

Boru lay couched, ignoring his companions, his big head set between the extended pasterns, facing the hills that lay beyond the flat where the circus tents were pitched. The range, thickly set to timber line with pines, green-black in the late afternoon light, brown where fire had scarred the forest, purple on the higher, more distant ridges; lifted up to snowy crests where one high peak pyramided above the rest.

Along the base of the foothills ran an emerald fringe of aspens. The cold gleam of a river separated the hills from Tamarack Flat, set with gray sagebrush and rabbitbush furred with golden bloom.

The heat of the day was passing, and the breeze blew cool from the range. Boru's trusty sentinels were alert. His eyes surveyed unblinkingly the scene before him, and ears and nose were keen to record the scents and sounds of this outside, new world. Down from the snowfields, through the pines, and across the flat wandered the wind, charged with a medley of odors and noises, telling to the initiate the story of the wild and the creatures that lived there. But to these, Boru, whose travel had been confined to baggage cars and his exercise of late to city streets, was a novice, haunted by conflicting emotions, vague suggestions of forgotten things, stirring within the dark chambers of his brain; a leaven of inherent impulse and experience.

Boru seldom deliberately remembered. Usually scent, sound, or revision supplied the motive power that started the review. The events of the last twenty-four hours had been so bewildering that his overcharged intellect flicked off its impressions at seeming random, swiftly forming mental pictures that ran back to far beyond the days when Holdini had bought him and bound him to vaudeville apprenticeship.

As he watched the rosy glow of the sunset creeping to the summit of the high peak, there came from somewhere the remembrance of someone—a woman—he had been glad to serve and who had made much of him. Coupled with this was a vision of himself lying on a bench in a great hall, with the yelping and barking of a thousand dogs of fifty breeds all about.

If he had understood more of man talk he would have learned long ago from Holdini's boasting that he was "Champion Boru of Stone Ridge," winner of cups and ribbons in many classes at the Madison Square Show, adjudged the best Irish wolfhound in America, and purchased by Holdini when the Stone Ridge Kennels were broken up by the illness of their owner, the mistress he had loved, who had gone West to recover from the cough that threatened her.

All that was a long time ago, as dog days run, and the impressions had been long dormant. Nowadays he saw no man he would willingly call master, few for whom he felt any sense of friendship. Dempsey was one of the latter. He remembered the kindly, intimate touch of the trainer's hand. Then the meeting with the wolf focused upon his mental screen, and his hair lifted as he bared his gums at the remembrance, while the saliva of longing for a fight again flooded his lower jaw, as a boy's mouth will water at the thought of green apples.

The rest of the dogs were peacefully asleep, oblivious of their surroundings, unconscious of the summons of the hills that seemed to Boru to call him imperatively, to awaken a longing that grew every moment more persistent in its urge to break his bondage, leaving the tricks he despised to see what lay within the forest and beyond the ridges, where so many things were stirring, unseen, barely hinted to scent and hearing, yet strangely familiar to some sixth sense within him.

Dempsey, a little unsteady of step and thick of speech, came around the tent and paused to speak.

"It's thinking you'd rather be free to roam the woods to-night," he said, "than playin' the fool for a lot of Reubens. An' ye're right, boy, ye're right. I'd like to go with ye, but I'm overcivilized, an' I need my comforts. Whisht, Boru, smell that, an' pleasant dreams to ye."

He tossed down an old, worn-out glove, one that he used when working around the cages. The smell of the beasts was strong upon it. It fell close to Boru's paws, and he held it between them as in a vise, growling in his throat.

When Dempsey looked back, laughing, Boru was worrying the glove with vicious snarls.

The big tent was filled from floor to slant of canvas roof with lumberjacks on their way to the spring camp, cowmen from the ranches of the big valley at the head of which Tamarack lay and with all the townsfolk old enough to sit up and see the performance. The size of the gate receipts had put Bilton in high good humor that extended to Holdini. The latter's only anxiety lay with the success of his act. He was doubtful of the effect of a demonstrative crowd on all sides of his dogs, accustomed only to a view of an audience over the footlights.

The performers were old friends with many of the good-natured crowd, who hailed them by their surnames. In the grand entry, the Countess Vladoska—Mrs. Bilton—bowed to the plaudits that greeted her appearance and graciously kissed a bouquet of somewhat wilted wild columbines and shooting-stars tossed to her by a blond giant, half her own age, but the acknowledged leader of the logging district.

The show opened well. The jests of the clowns were fervently appreciated, the gymnasts writhed and the tight-rope performers balanced to cheers and, when La Petite Cora—Mrs. Bilton's sister—aged thirty-six and looking at most eighteen, bounded gracefully through the hoops from the back of her placid mount, she broke the hearts of a dozen admirers for every tissue circle that she pierced.

Boru awaited his turn in a corner of the dressing tent, lying by the paraphernalia of the act. The rest of the dog performers showed their excitement by restless movements and glad yaps and barks subdued by Holdini's sharp commands. Boru lay with his head on his forepaws, awaiting the signal, impatient for the act to be over. The taste and scent of Dempsey's glove was still strong in his mouth, and he wanted to be undisturbed so that he could retire into himself and let the strange ferment he felt quickening within him come to some understanding with his consciousness.

From the big tent came the smell of close-packed humanity, the tang of the ring sprinkled with fresh sawdust, the odor of horses. Under the flap of the dressing tent stole the cool night wind, redolent with the perfume of sage and pine, mysterious with hints to which he felt momentarily more strangely kin.

A man took the signal from Bilton, perspiring in befrogged coat and riding breeches as ringmaster; Holdini nodded to his attendants, and they hurried out with the planks and barrels and low hurdles that were the properties of the act. The dogs, unleashed, trailed Houdini into the ring, the smaller ones frolicking with shrill barks; a big Newfoundland, dressed as a clown, gamboling clumsily, and the great Danes ambling to their stations with lolling tongues and eager, shifting eyes. Boru followed more sedately.

"Hey, look at the big gray wolf," shouted a woodsman, and the lumber-jacks surveyed him with a special interest that he ignored, gazing with half-closed eyes at the pert poodles and terriers going self-consciously through their tricks.

TOGETHER WITH A BIG NEWFOUNDLAND, DRESSED AS A CLOWN ;
A GREAT DANE, AND A PERT POODLE, BORU WATCHED THE
TERRIER GOING, SELF-CONSCIOUSLY, THROUGH HIS TRICKS

The act, with a few minor mishaps, proceeded smoothly to the last triumphant tableau. Holdini struck an attitude, the crowd clapped hearty commendation, and the Canine Circus achieved a successful entry into Circusdom.

At a crack of the whip, the dogs left the ring to make way for a tumbling act. In the dressing tent, Holdini gave them their reward of raw meat, well satisfied with himself. He offered to pat Boru, but the wolfhound avoided the caress, lying down apart.

The act of the Countess Vladoska and the wolves was featured between the two rings, emptied of confusing attractions. The four brutes were brought on in a cage barred on all four sides, into which they had been herded by Dempsey, supperless, to render them more tractable in the knowledge that their meal awaited their successful performance. But the unappeased appetites made them restless, and the imagination of the audience supplied the suggestion of ferocity announced on the lithographs. Mrs. Bilton, as the countess, appeared in a fur-trimmed costume, supposed to be that of a hussar, with tights ornamented with gold braid—a little tarnished—a shako of fur upon her black hair, a jaunty cape swung from one shoulder.

"The countess," announced Bilton; "in her mar-vel-ous control of these fee-ro-cious brutes whose habits and crew-el-ty are so well known to this dis-ting-wished audience, has

succeeded—and she alone—in sub-du-ing their natural fear
of the fi-e-ry element. I will ask for si-lence during the
per-form-ance, every moment of which is fraught with peril
to the exhibitor of these vicious man-eaters."

The women and children in the audience shuddered a little, and the men reassured them. Then, as the music
stopped, the countess, a pistol in her belt, a short whip in
her hand, slipped through the door that Dempsey held open
and motioned the four wolves to their low platforms in the
corners of the cage.

The wolves were stupid performers compared with the
dogs, but their act was more spectacular, including, true
to the pictured promise of the placards, leaps through fiery
hoops.

Something more than hunger affected them. Their
meeting with Boru had left them with nerves on edge with
the arousing of hatred, as it had the dog, and they worked
sullenly, with shifty eyes and spasmodic wrinkling of their
lips, and suggestive licking of their chops with furtive
tongues.

Dempsey, half drunk as he was, was the first to notice
the uneasiness of the wolves. Bilton saw it next, and,
edging close to the cage, threw an aside to his wife to hurry
the performance and to be wary of the always uncertain
tempers of the beasts.

Bilton, not altogether justly, blamed Dempsey for their condition. Aside from the meeting with Boru, the proximity of the wilderness invariably infected the whole menagerie with the same restless longing for freedom that was puzzling the wolfhound.

The countess put the wolves imperatively through their paces, marking every protest with the menace of her whip. The wolves snarlingly posed, with her as the center of the group, using one as a couch, her arms about two more, the fourth submissive at her feet, the whip between his jaws.

In the dressing tent, Boru, unleashed, crouched upright, close to the canvas alleyway that led to the main tent. Suddenly he sprang to his feet, the coarse hair lifting about his neck and along his spine, his ears raised, his nostrils wide, quivering from muzzle to tail tip as the scent of the wolves worked through the maze of circus odors and came, faint, but unmistakable, to where he lay.

Unnoticed, on padded feet, his head forward and lowered, his short mane bristling and with eyes afire, he stole forward until he stood unseen at the performers' entrance, eager for a sight of his enemy. Boru's scent, all uncultivated as it was, was not his strongest ally. His eyes first, his ears next, were the keenest of his senses. Later he was to develop all of them.

It had taken time for the wolf smell to penetrate the conflicting scents of the big tent.   As Boru's eyes searched the circus arena, Dempsey put through the bars of the performing cage the open hoops bound with waste fresh dipped in alcohol, through which the wolves leaped to conclude the act.

The countess, her eyes on the restless brutes, took the hoops and reached a hand back of her for the torch with which to light them.   Things had reached a critical stage. The wolf which had held the whip had refused to give it up willingly, and at the sight of the hoops and the smell of the alcohol, the four backed snarlingly into their corners, with mouths agape.

Boru heard the snarls and crept slowly forward.   His sight was obscured for the moment by the border of the first ring, and he circled it as the countess forced the first wolf to leap through the flaming hoop.   A second followed.   The two she-wolves refused point-blank, and remained on their corner platforms, showing their fangs.   The countess pluckily lashed them with her whip, forcing them at last to make the jump, though the alcohol had evaporated and the fire was dead.

Boru growled as he came around the ring into full sight of the cage.   The wolves broke into sudden howls, menacing the woman with their evident determination to dispute her authority, and to take up the challenge of Boru.

The audience began to shift uneasily. Bilton, his crimson face turned purple with excitement and terror, called to his wife to leave the cage. She retreated to the bars, felt for the spring catch, fired her blank cartridges right and left at the wolves, and slipped her body through the narrowly opened door.

A gasp of relief went up from the benches, followed by a groan as a braided loop of her cape caught on the latch. She put up a hand swiftly to free herself, and at the same instant one of the wolves sprang, striking her on the breast, wrenching free the braid and hurling the countess through the door to fall defenseless on the sawdust. A second wolf followed. The remaining two leaped simultaneously from the other side of the cage, their bodies meeting in mid-air and slamming the door automatically fast in the impact.

Bilton rushed to the aid of his prostrate wife, over whom stood the dog wolf. Dempsey felt in his pocket for the emergency automatic that should have been there, and cursed when his hand encountered only his flask. He picked up the whip that had fallen outside the cage and belabored the wolf about the muzzle as it snapped and snarled, too confused by the attack to worry the fallen woman. The she-wolf stood snarling between the two rings.

Shrieks rang through the tent above the cries of the

men. The benches began to give way as the frightened people fought to reach the main exit. Some of the men leaped the barrier and hurried across the ring to aid in the rescue, while the circus attendants and roustabouts came running in with steel goads and improvised weapons.

But Boru forestalled them. A great gray shape, with eyes aflame and jaws wide apart, hurtled through the air. The startled she-wolf crouched as his last leap brought him above her, then sprang upward, slashing with scissor jaws at Boru's belly. She was the fraction of a second too late. The hound's shoulder struck her chest with a driving force and weight that sent her rolling on her back. A second more and the she-wolf lay a huddled mass, her throat torn out, disemboweled by one tearing rip, and Boru rushed on to take toll of the foe his new-found fighting spirit had longed to meet since they first glared at each other with instinctive hate.

There was not an ounce of cowardice in the ninety-odd pounds of the dog-wolf's body, but he was bewildered with the sting of the whip Dempsey plied, the blows that Bilton hammered on his skull with the emergency bar of iron, and the sight of twenty men closing in on him. For a moment his heart faltered at the death cry of his mate and the sight of Boru's bloody muzzle and gleaming fangs. The odds were too great. He turned tail and sped for present safety.

Boru whirled in pursuit, following straight for the main exit, already partly choked by the hysterical crowd. The frightened folk made way for them. Screaming, a woman fell, and her rescuers formed a temporary barrier behind the wolf, barring Boru. With a roar, he leaped the struggling heap and raced after his quarry, gaining at every leap as they tore across the moonlit flat toward the hills.

The full moon had risen, and its cold brilliance, added to the steely glitter of the clustering stars, flooded the flat with a soft radiance that sharply defined the sage clumps, each with its pool of purple shadow widening as the moon lifted. In the half light, Boru followed the wolf's urgent lope unerringly, the two beasts racing toward the river like gray ghosts, their pads noiseless on the soil.

The wolf was seven years old. He was a gray timber wolf, captured, as Dempsey shrewdly guessed, in Montana. That had happened two years ago, not long enough for him to forget the hardly learned tricks of offensive and defensive fighting, the scars of which marked his body beneath the shaggy fur. But he was fat from over-feeding, or Boru would have had little chance against the veteran of a hundred fights.

Both were out of condition from lack of exercise but at first sight Boru seemed to hold a great advantage in size and weight. The wolf was scarcely thirty inches at the shoulders against Boru's thirty-six, and the dog outweighed him by almost forty pounds.

But it was veteran against novice, woods master against tenderfoot, professional against amateur. Boru's strength had not been trained to coördination with a brain stored with the best of all fighting allies—experience.

The wolf was a past master at the war game. As they raced, his crafty, treacherous eyes rolled far back to judge the nearness of Boru, then roved ahead in the hope of finding an open space in the sage, where he could bring into play his tactics of swift inleap and out again, cut and slash and dodge. He had neither the intention nor the desire to come to close quarters with Boru; but, once free of outside interference, he had little fear of the outcome. He and his mate had more than once proven a match for a bear. Had she been with him, the combination would have spelled quick disaster for Boru.

Boru had no fighting plans. He was consumed with blind fury, handicapped from overconfidence after his speedy victory over the surprised she-wolf. In great, driving leaps, eighteen feet to a bound, he overhauled the wolf on the right flank, intent upon reaching the shoulder and crunching into the vertebræ of the neck. While they galloped the wolf circled always to the left in a great curve, straining every effort to reach open ground, and avoid a rough-and-tumble fight among the sage.

Boru had come into his own. Through his veins the blood coursed joyfully. Through his rage a sense of freedom exalted him. He had tasted blood. The old life was behind him. The scent of his enemy was in his nostrils, his body almost within reach of his jaws. Twice he snapped viciously and missed as the wolf swerved, then bounded on with renewed determination, his heart pounding his ribs, following the wolf through the maze of sagebrush, panting, resolute, filled with the desire to kill.

The sage grew more sparsely as they reached the end of the flat where the river separated it from the first foot-hills, and here and there were spaces of open ground.

The wolf had heard the click of Boru's teeth and had felt them as they met in the folds of his neck, tearing away fur and skin. It was time for the rally. His quick eye sighted a gully a little way ahead, where the rains had worn a course in the soft soil. Now it was dust dry, about two feet in depth. He made three or four desperate bounds and landed, crouching in the ditch, regaining his feet swiftly, doubling on his tracks as Boru, unable to break his leap, sprang over him.

On the farther edge of the gully, Boru, bewildered at the sudden move, whirled, to find his foe facing him on the opposite side. Roaring his war bark, he hurled himself across the depression.

His jaws clashed on air as the wolf, swerving, leaped swiftly in and back out of reach. Boru felt the rip of teeth at his shoulder, though he was unconscious of pain or of the blood flowing from the gash. Again he rushed and missed. Time after time the wolf eluded him, and Boru found himself at last the hub of a series of attacks, facing the circling brute that shuttled in and out too swiftly for him to counter successfully. There were four rips on his shoulders now, and, try as he would, he could not come to grips. His thoughts of a furious mêlée in which he would rend his enemy to pieces by sheer strength vanished.

The wolf was in his element, master at his own game. It was the fight of the thrasher against the whale, of rapier against bludgeon. The vivid moonlight gave ample light for the combat.

Once Boru found an opening. As his adversary darted in, twisting his snaky neck to slash, Boru lunged furiously, the force of the collision tossing the wolf aside. Boru struck for the loins, and the wolf turned with a snarl at the grip of the viselike jaws before he tore free at the penalty of a raw wound.

So far the struggle had been noiseless, save for their panting. Now they fought with guttural sounds of rage deep in their gullets. Once, Boru, adopting his opponent's tactics of attack with forward jump and quick retreat after a ripping stroke, felt his quarters slide into the little gully. The wolf, following up the opening, sprang for his throat. Boru's heavy collar, badge of the servitude he had discarded, saved him. The wolf's teeth tore through the leather, clashing against the heavy brass studs and failing to gain the grip that, once established, would have ended the battle.

Boru's blind rage had gone with a growing respect for the craft of his foe, and the slip into the ditch gave him a plan of action. He was beginning to fight with his head. The wolf was getting badly winded and his dazzling attack less bewildering. His failure to grip the wolfhound's throat made him wary of repeating the attempt. Instead, he tried to snap at Boru's pasterns and sever the tendons. The weight of the wolfhound made him careful. Had it been another wolf he would have been surer of his mode of battle.

Boru commenced once more to assume the offensive, charging open-mouthed, inviting attack. Then, as the wolf gave ground and leaped in again, he turned, taking the attack on his forequarter, where the sharp teeth could reach no vulnerable point and only gashed the shallow flesh on ribs and shoulder blade, thrusting the wolf back by the sheer impetus of his own superior strength and poundage, backing him gradually toward the depression.

The wolf despised Boru as an amateur, though he was afraid of his bulk, and gave way craftily before the desperate onrush, snarling and darting in to gouge with his chiseled fangs. The shadowed gully lay like a bar of purple across the open space, and Boru measured the distance in his charges. He felt the rip-rap of the wolf's teeth as they met, ivory to bone, against his ribs, with mounting anger. But the fight mist had cleared from his eyes, and he battled on with a definite purpose.

At last they were on the edge of the gully, and Boru, dripping with blood that tangled his coat, drove onward. The wolf leaped backward and found no foothold, rolling at the bottom of the shallow ditch. Boru plunged downward, driving his muzzle through the kicking forelegs, pinning down the struggling body, and wrenching his teeth through the gristly windpipe.

A havoc of worrying snarls followed. The gray dust of the gully lifted and hid the combatants. When it settled again, Boru stood astraddle of his enemy, now a lifeless, though still palpitating mass; torn to shapelessness in the final, desperate rally.

Boru lapped the warm blood from the torn throat as it puddled on the sandy soil, watched for a quiver of returning vigor, then leaped out of the gully. He was not hungry.   He had not yet learned the lesson of the wild, to eat when and where one could, for fear of to-morrow's abstinence.   The fury of the fight was over.   Vaguely he missed a gallery.   There was no one to acknowledge the victory so hardly won.

He stood on the edge of the arroyo, looking down at the huddle that a moment before had been a leaping, biting hazard of his life and exulted in the conquest.   The world of vaudeville and circus seemed very far away.   He had achieved freedom, fought for it, won it by his own strength and cunning, and he had no mind to relinquish it.

Suddenly his ears lifted.   Through the night came faint sounds that threatened his newly achieved independence.

Bilton and his men, striving to quiet the audience, had managed to prevent a panic, but a score of volunteers had joined Holdini and Dempsey, who had sprung on two of the circus horses and started in pursuit of Boru and the wolf.   The cowboys mounted, eager to display their courage.   Tamarack was in no mood to have a wolf loitering on its outskirts and, to most of the audience, Boru was an equal enemy to sound sleep of nights.   The lumbermen followed on foot, armed with clubs and here and there with a rifle or a revolver.

Boru raised his head and stood at gaze, still panting too heavily from the fight to distinguish sounds, his eyes fixed on lights that danced far across the flat where the circus tents glowed like gigantic lanterns.

The lights came rapidly toward him, and he could hear the shouts of men urging each other on. The gallop of the ponies' hoofs was soon distinguishable, and for a moment he hesitated. Instinct prompted him to run, custom suggested that he had nothing to fear from men.

A horse galloped swiftly down a lane between the bushes, and the figure on its back tossed up one arm and shouted. The next second Boru saw a red flash split the darkness, something buzzed past his head with the drone of an angry insect and thudded dully into the ground. He wheeled as the next shot was fired and ran unscathed, for the river. The man's yell was taken up, and Boru, as he ran, leaping the clumps of sage in his stride, sensed the chase converging upon him and knew himself the quarry.

Driven by the shouts behind him, Boru raced for the water, intent upon gaining the refuge of the hills beyond the river, bewildered by the sudden hue and cry, astounded at finding himself a hunted fugitive, but resolute for freedom. As he neared the bank where the winter storm-waters had cut through the soft earth of the flat, three horsemen pounded along to his right, threatening to cut him off. He reached the edge first, looking down to the fifty-foot drop that caused him to swerve and follow alcng the bank for an easier descent. The ground was practically bare of brush, and as the forces of his pursuers once more joined, they raised a view halloo at sight of Boru, sorely winded now, striving in desperate leaps to win to safety.

"Don't shoot, you fool! It's the dog. Look at his ears."

Boru's ears were those of a collie, and the wolf's erect and pointed. The distinction was clear in the moonlight, and Holdini's voice arrested the cowboy's lifted hand and halted the finger on the trigger.

"Head him off!" shouted Holdini. "There's fifty dollars in it if we get him back to camp."

The two were ahead of the rest of the riders. The man thrust his gun into its holster and fumbled with the rope that hung coiled from his saddle.

"I'll get him," he said. The next moment he was swinging his lariat in a widening loop above his head as he set spurs to his blown pony for a last spurt.

Boru, close to the bank, heard the hastening tumult of the hoofs, and cast a backward glance, visioning the waving arm that suddenly straightened as it tossed the lariat in unerring aim.

The lithe rope swished through the air as the coils straightened. Before Boru, the circle of the noose showed like a thin loop. He realized its menace, and, with a desperate bound, sprang clear through the loop that just grazed his tucked-up hind quarters.

The man swore as he recoiled his rope, and Holdini echoed him. A jeer came from the nearest riders who had seen the futile throw.

Boru was in hard straits; the last leap seemed to have robbed him of the end of the strength that had been filtering from him as he ran. There was no spring to his loins, his muscles ached, and his legs were stiffening, his lungs were burning, his throat a torment. He looked desperately to where the water ran gray and sullen fifty feet below with the swirl of the current showing gray against the rocks, like the fangs of a fresh enemy.

The two horsemen were close upon him, racing parallel with his course and the banks of the river, threatening to head him off, and, with the rest of the cavalcade, herd him back into the sage, where, in his exhaustion, he could not hope to avoid capture.

The cowboy's pony thundered alongside, the man swinging his rope like a lash, too close for another attempt with the loop. Despairingly Boru twisted and plunged between the startled pony's legs, slashing at the hocks as he leaped clear. The horse reared, and the angry rider, dropping the rope, drew his gun, and, despite Holdini's protestations, fired.

"He's no better'n a wolf," he shouted. "Tried to hamstring my hawss, damn him!"

The bullets thudded into the soil about Boru as he doubled back for the river, summoning his last ounce of energy. He fled past the riders directly in front of the plunging hoofs, and, regardless of the fifty-foot leap, hurled himself over the bank.

He smashed under the water in a smother of foam, and came to the surface, striking out in desperation. Like others of his wiry coat, he naturally hated water. He had never been in it beyond the depth of his pasterns before, and swimming was an untested talent, but the shock of the cool water of the pool into which he had plunged revived him, momentarily renewing his strength. His great chest held his head and shoulders high, and he found his powerful strokes sending him swiftly forward toward the opposite shore.

A wake of white water trailed him as he swam, making a mark of him in the moonlight at which the men fired, unmindful of Holdini's pleas. They had dismounted for better aim, and the bullets spattered viciously about the hound as he forged onward.

As Boru reached the wilder current in the center of the stream it was hard for the marksmen to distinguish him amid the smother of foam. The men with the rifles had not come up, and the range was too far for accurate revolver firing. The shooting became desultory, then ceased, as the disgusted pursuers lost sight of Boru in the foam-streaked rapids.

But Boru faced a graver danger than the random bullets. The river, still swollen by the late spring thaws, ran furiously in mid-channel, chafing among the bowlders, swirling in eddies that swept the tired dog, at their will, with irresistible force. Once the surge jammed him against a great rock and held him there, struggling to keep his head above water, powerless for the moment until a little strength returned to him in the face of the imminent peril. A submerged bowlder carried his legs from under him, and he was whirled helpless, rolled like a log until another more friendly rock aided him to get his muzzle above water and get air to his lungs.

Half drowned, he fought his way through the mid-stream turmoil, swam weakly across a quieter pool, and found bottom for his toes at last. He dragged himself out upon a strip of firm sand that lay between the water and the aspens and lay prone. His dark, limp form showed plainly on the white river sand, and a flash came from the shore

he had left, a rifle bullet sang past and plunged ahead of
him, spurting into the beach.   Somewhere he found vitality
for a last effort and crawled into the high brake beneath
the aspens, hauling himself deep into the shelter of the brush
to lie breathless, a water-soaked bedraggled mass, too tired
to stir, seemingly lifeless.

He lay there for an hour while the moon climbed the
ridges, heedless of his wounds smarting from the water,
careless of his stiffening limbs, emancipated, but an outlaw.
Man, up till now, if not his friend, at least showing him
good will, had turned against him.   He accepted the situation.   Henceforth he would avoid humanity.   He could
fend for himself.   If man had no use for him, neither had
he need of man.

Presently he rose on stiff legs, shook his shaggy coat,
and stretched himself.   He was thirsty, but he dared not
return to the river.   He set his face to the hills that
mounted to the snowy, pyramidal peak, and, as action set
his blood stirring and took the cramp from his limbs, trotted
on and up into his new domain.

The gashes from the wolf's sharp teeth were stiffening
on Boru's shoulders as he breasted the second ridge.   He
had barely noticed them in the exploration of this wonder-
land of the pines where a thousand subtle scents and noises
seemed to hail him as one coming into his own.   Forms

unseen, unknown, scuttered away through the bush; here and there he caught the glint of eyes; once a great owl floated over him, hooting as it soared on noiseless wings. But none disputed his passages; he seemed to have come among his own people.

Gradually, as his eyes grew more accustomed to the woods, he noted the growing light, and wondered at it. Now, as he topped the rise, the mystery solved itself in the circle of the moon that broke through the apparent tangle of brushwood and soared clear of the lifting range, lighting the snowy pyramid of the topmost peak.

Boru sat back on his haunches at the sight. In the fury of the chase, the battle, and the flight, the moon had not affected him. Now, within him, subconsciously, his spirit vibrated and made itself manifest in a long, undulating howl. Something in the sight of the full, golden circle impelled the outburst. Though Boru failed to sense it, it was the old cry, the rally of the hunters, the call to muster. Under the radiance, deer and smaller game were moving, and those who preyed sounded the call to each other over ridge and valley. It was the "Hullali" of the open, the greeting of the wild.

"Good hunting, brother!" was the meaning of the cry, inspired by the mounting moon. Boru sounded it again, and

instinctively waited for a response. It was another part
of his unused heritage—the password of the pack.

There was no answer. The echoes of the call trumpeted
between the ridges. A myriad rustlings, almost inaudible,
told of the suspension of activities by the lesser night folk
of fur and feather. The moon lifted slowly, and Boru
bayed to it, haunched down, his throat extended, his muzzle, bloodied with his victories, upthrust to the zenith.

The brook, far below, suddenly caught a moonbeam and
reflected it in a flash of silver. Boru's thirst revived. He
had had neither time nor thought of drinking when he
swam the river, and this new world of the piny ridges, with
their suggestion of present and future adventure, had for a
time offset the fever of the fight. But the sudden shimmer
of the stream roused an imperative desire to slake his
parched throat. He padded downward to the stream and
drank his fill before he climbed the upslope of the third
ridge. Near the top, he came upon a rabbit which had
ventured out to feed and failed to scent or hear alarm until
the last, fateful moment. As it crouched ready for flight,
ears set at the danger signal, Boru came from the shadows,
twisting a snaky neck as the rabbit, leaping the tenth of
a second too late, squealed a vain protest.

In the novelty of combat, Boru, full-stomached before

the fight, had disdained the carcass of the wolf. But this was a titbit, and he bolted his kill. The flavor of this reward of his own prowess, still warm, the sudden excitement of finding the game, the swift, sure snap, the crunch of teeth through quivering, full-blooded flesh, all were a fresh initiation into this new independence he had achieved.

At the top of the ridge, the moon met him full again. He shifted his eyes from its brilliance. Far down the valley a light twinkled, fixed and steady, the sign of man's habitation and man's control of the invincible weapon— fire. It meant little to Boru at present except a place to be avoided. Fire to him thus far had always been a friend. Now he vaguely associated it with the red spurts in the darkness that had been followed by the stinging, thudding bullets that had threatened him.

The wind blew gently down the long funnel of the draw. On it was borne a vibrant essence that filled Boru's nostrils with a strange delight, penetrating to a region of his brain that thrilled to the mysterious influence. Boru had met one great primal force since Dempsey had taken him to the cages in the menagerie—the lust for blood, both in the battle and for food; now the greatest force of all gripped him with elemental power—sex.

Somewhere in the dusky ravine below was a mate, ripe for conquest. Loneliness took possession of him, then long-

BORU WAS IN HARD STRAITS; THE LAST LEAP SEEMED TO
HAVE ROBBED HIM OF THE END OF THE STRENGTH THAT HAD
BEEN FILTERING FROM HIM AS HE RAN

ing. Still erect, he snuffed the breeze and sounded a cry that mocked the resistance of the wind. It was not the summons of the pack this time; it was the bugle call of love, at once an invitation and a challenge to any one who dared dispute his right of summons.

From upwind there came an answering note. In the darkness some one waited his wooing. With eyes sparkling, ears uplifted, his tail carried like a banner, Boru took up the love trail.

CHAPTER TWO

MATING

THE thicket that grew beneath the pines on the brow of the cañon slope was transformed by the magic of the moonlight into a silver and ebony tangle of light and shade, shifting and quivering as the breeze moved the leaves and lighter branches. On the edge of the thicket stood Boru, his gray coat almost invisible in the half light, silent and motionless, seemingly as much a part of the inanimate landscape as the trees and shrubbery.

But beneath the apparent rigidity of his great bulk every nerve quivered with eagerness, every sense played the rôle of alert sentinel as the wolfhound listened, looked, and snuffed the wind for a response to the call he had sounded. His collie-like ears were lifted, his eyes luminous in the shadow, and the end of his long muzzle, with the moist nostrils distended, twitching from side to side. His long jaws were agape, and between them his eager tongue vibrated, poised between the gleaming teeth.

It was spring; the sap was mounting in the trees, and with the unfolding of the buds the animate creatures of the wild were obeying the summons of the mating instinct. Although kennel bred, his life so far spent in taking an unwelcome part in the performances of Holdini's Canine Circus, this world of the woods, so new to Boru, had suddenly become familiar. A few hours before he had been a cog in the circus machine, a slave to the length of his leash and the regularity of his meals. Then Dempsey, the drunken ex-trainer, had shown him the caged wolves and awakened the impulses inherent in his spirit and breeding that had lain so long dormant within him. All that, and his successful bid for freedom with its mêlée of fight and flight, was for the time forgotten. Boru had an infinite capacity for concentration upon the one present purpose.

Through the night the wind still brought to him the message of the mysterious, penetrating essence that had thrilled and excited him, invoking a sudden sense of loneliness, dominating him with the stirring of sex. Boru upthrust his muzzle, straining his throat as, with forelegs set wide apart, he sounded his love call once again.

For the moment there was no audible answer, though the air held the mute assurance that his quest was well founded. Then the reply came back as if in tardy echo, a cry unpromising, yet provocative.

Boru tingled to the teasing challenge of it. He forgot the wounds still raw upon his shoulders where the fangs of the dog wolf had raked him, forgot the stiffness of his limbs, the weariness of his muscles. All his energies were fired afresh, and he was conscious only of the desire to pursue and overtake the mysterious, unknown mate who waited for him in the darkness.

He trotted clear of the thicket, and stood for a moment on the bowlder of a rocky outcrop, trying to decide upon his direction, then plunged downhill, crashing through the brushwood, overleaping obstacles, until at last he broke through a mass of fragrant fern that bordered a strip of grassland beside a tinkling stream. In the center of the little meadow stood an animal, white-furred, showing like a gray ghost in the gloom of the cañon bottom, where the moonbeams had not yet penetrated. It was a white she-wolf. She stood with ears erect, listening to the impetuous rush of Boru down the hillside. Her shaggy brush waved gently to and fro as she waited for the wooer who had announced his intentions by his deep-throated signal.

Boru bounded into the open, and, with a glad, low bark of greeting, sped toward her. He did not stop to consider whether she was dog of his own kind or wolf of his enemies' breed. It would have made no difference. The instinct of hatred was dulled by that of sex. His muzzle still held stains of the blood of two of her race, but he had killed them in the fury of a mutual fighting lust. Now gentler impulses prevailed. The wizardry of mating overrode all question of blood and breed.

In Boru's eyes the white she-wolf was beautiful. To her Boru's great bulk, far bigger than that of her own kind, coming toward her with great, masterful leaps, seemed the embodiment of an ideal mate. But, being feminine, and true to her instincts, she was in no mood for quick surrender. For a few moments she stood gazing at Boru as he came on, a little frightened at the great size of him, sensing immediately that he was an alien, yet already resolved to take him as mate and at the same time prove herself no easy conquest.

Her own unusual and conspicuous color, though not extremely rare, had set her aside from the rest of her own pack, brown wolves all of them, and although three years old she had never mated. This spring was indeed the first season at which the mating impulse had overwhelmingly affected her.

When Boru reached the spot where two more leaps would have brought him to her side, she whirled and raced off at the top of her speed. Boru followed in swift pursuit, giving tongue in low, deep-chested barks to convince her that he came in love and not in war. He saw the roll of her eyes as the she-wolf turned her head to watch him while she raced, and his spirit caught the infection of the love chase.

As he overhauled her and thrust his muzzle caressingly against her shoulder she halted suddenly and leaped sidewise, so that they stood for a moment with their moist noses almost touching, their breaths mingling, Boru's dark-brown eyes wooing the she-wolf's greenish-amber orbs. With quick jumps she kept her front to him until, watchful of her opportunity, she raced away once more, Boru beside her, snapping at him in playful dalliance as they made the circuit of the little meadow. The lifting moon had topped the pines of the ridge and turned the arena of their love-making to a pool of silver.

The she-wolf turned, and, reaching the center of the meadow, lay down, panting, while Boru gamboled in front of her with free-thrown forelegs, showing off his paces, advancing and retreating, as she watched him appraisingly and approvingly. Gradually he grew closer in his approach and gently nuzzled her, biting softly at her ears, while she made little snarls of mock protest. Then he lay down beside her, his long head close to hers, his tongue caressing her. She turned and nipped him.

A wandering cloudlet floated over the moon. The meadow's silver swiftly tarnished. She jumped to her feet, and loped, Boru beside her, to the sweet-scented shadows of the fern brake.

The moon disentangled itself and showed the fern fronds noddingly proclaiming the secret of the bower where the wild lovers had hidden their love-making. The breeze, in sudden sympathy, ruffled all the ferns and sped onward a great mass of cloud that effectually obscured the shining planet.

The moon had almost completed its curve of duty for the night, and was sinking once more behind the hills as Boru and his mate trotted into a clearing where a forest fire had felled the pines, leaving only a few gaunt, blackened poles upstanding to the stars. Crossing the gap, leaping over the prostrate timber, they reached a bench thickset with dogwood, and, penetrating the thicket, looked down upon the river that ran between the foothills and the sage-covered plain of Tamarack Flat. Across the Flat appeared the sleeping town of Tamarack and vaguely gray in the distance, the big tents of the circus from which Boru had achieved his emancipation.

Nebulous above the dormant town hung the light haze that is to be found above the gathered habitations of man, and the dirty white sides of the tents swayed slightly in the breezing night air.

They sat down on their haunches, their tongues lolling from their jaws. They had climbed and crossed three ridges from the little valley of their love-making, the wolf following Boru's long lope as he led the way back toward the place where he had won his first fight, anxious to show his mate the carcass of the wolf, first to establish his prowess as protector, next to assuage the hunger that beset both of them.

Boru's bold eyes roved over the scene. He was looking for an easier crossing at the river than the turbulent passage he had made, pursued by the men who sought to return him to his old captivity, or, failing that, to kill him as an equal menace with the wolf that had escaped from the training cage in the circus arena and which he had overtaken and killed close to the bank of the river.

He still held a keen recollection of the red flashes that had suddenly blossomed in the dark behind him, the sharp reports, and the thud of the bullets that had so narrowly missed him, but instinct and experience both taught him that the night was the time when man relaxed his dominion, and sight and sound and scent reassured him that there was little to fear from his recent masters.

As they squatted side by side, the difference between them was marked. Boru was half as heavy again as his mate of the wilderness. His shoulders topped hers by half a dozen inches, his gray, crisp hair was shorter and coarser, his ears were those of a collie, while hers pricked sharply upward; his head was blunter, and his tail, compared with her plumy brush, almost scraggly. But he admired her as his eyes rested on her as she stood up to stretch and yawn, bowing her head between her forelegs and giving him a

IN BORU'S EYES, THE WHITE SHE-WOLF WAS BEAUTIFUL

wifely nip before she haunched down again beside him, obediently awaiting his initiative.

She was not a true albino. Her eyes retained the usual golden green of her tribe. She was perfectly white, as snowy as an arctic fox. Long-nosed, she weighed about seventy pounds and was about as tall as a greyhound, slim beneath her long, shaggy fur in distinction to the muscular bulk of the Irish wolfhound. Her mouth was split far back and heavy through the butt of the jaw, her gleaming tusks long and ivory white, her upstanding ears full four inches long. Like Boru, she was deep of chest, well cut up in the flanks, and narrow through the body and hams. About her neck the fur was ruffled, almost amounting to a mane. Her feathery tail was well over a foot long; from tip to tip she measured two inches over five feet, ten inches less than her lord. Now her eyes glowed with the soft light of happy surrender as she gazed lovingly at Boru.

Boru rose and started swiftly down the slope, finding his way through the laurel and dense brush growth by the trails of deer and lesser animals whose quick surrender of their paths was made manifest by a hundred rustlings as they retreated before the pair. Once a pair of eyes glared at them from a clump of azalea, and a lynx, deeming discretion the better part of valor, backed away on padded paws. Halfway down to the river, a covey of sleepy grouse scattered in alarm and drummed off over the bushes out of reach, while the two gazed at them with jaws slavering from disappointed appetite.

They kept steadily downward, and passed through the belt of aspens that banked the river, emerging, after a cautious survey, upon the sandy margin of the torrent, still swollen from the spring melting of the mountain snows. Across the water the bluff, where the stream had worn its way through the soft soil of the plateau, dipped to the level of the stream that ran in swift shallows over its widened bed.

Gingerly, for they both disliked water save when necessity demanded passage, they splashed through the shallows and gained the flat, mounting up to its general level. Boru's sense of direction was good, though amateur as yet in application, but his leadership became uncertain as they reached the sage clumps. It was the she-wolf who picked up the trail and broke into a lope with Boru at her shoulder.

To the human understanding, weaned by civilization from the practices of necessity, the adventures of Boru and his mate held much of paradox. Boru's breeding for many years under its alliance with man had trained him to hate and hunt the wolf, yet, upon the call of the most powerful of all physical impulses—sex—he reverted for his mating to the clan with which, in long-past ages, he had

once claimed kinship.[1]   And his mate, still under the rul-
ing of the wild, held no compunction against sating her
hunger with the carcass of her own breed.   Nor were they
the first of their kind to follow their promptings.

The moon, clear-rimmed to the last, dropped reluctantly
behind the elbow of the main range, and, for the moment,
the cold stars seemed to gain greater brilliancy.   There
were still two hours before dawn, and the night was very
still.   The sage, relieved of their shadows by the with-
drawal of the moon, stood in purple clumps that seemed
solid in the obscurity rather than built up of twigs and
leaves, apparently merging into a solid mass in the center
of the plateau.   Between them the wild mates loped unerringly to the scene of Boru's encounter.

As they came at last to the place, twisting and severing
down the avenues of sage, Boru forged ahead, glimpsing
the form of his conquered adversary, a dull blotch on the
ground.   Other figures surrounded it, and Boru, with the
memory of his fight awakening, charged down upon the

[1] "The interbreeding of wolves with dogs bred by pioneers produced a
really worthy progeny. St. George Mivart has said 'hybrids between the
dog and the wolf have proved to be fertile, though for no long period.'
The writer remembers that in his early boyhood, about twenty years ago
(1894), he saw several of these wolf-dogs. They were intelligent and
kindly, and highly prized by their owners, farmers in some of the valleys
adjacent to the Seven Mountains. (Pennsylvania.)"—*Henry W. Shoe-
maker, Author of "Wolf Days in Pennsylvania," "Black Forest Souvenirs,"
et cetera.*

group wide-mouthed, sounding his guttural war-cry, his mate following hard upon his heels.

There was sudden constellation of green eyes glaring at Boru as he galloped in; then the dim shapes of half a dozen coyotes separated, bolting for cover in as many directions to the sheltering sage. Boru roared and rushed, but the cowardly beasts melted into the night, confusing him by their scattering disappearance, fleeing for safety from his threatening bulk on feet as swift as his own. He returned from the fruitless chase to meet his mate coming in from a tangent course equally unsuccessful.

The coyotes had practically finished their feast. There was little left of the gray timber wolf but a torn hide and scattered bones. Chagrined and winded, Boru sniffed the remnants and looked toward his mate shamefacedly. She, more used than he to the misadventures of meal gathering, took the matter nonchalantly, and, nuzzling his shoulder, started determinedly on the back trail. Boru glanced around the sage with lingering hopes of vengeance upon the coyotes, and followed her, recognizing the evident purpose of her steady lope toward the river. Intuitively he acknowledged her superior hunting craft and allowed her to take the lead, intent upon profiting by her lore.

The she-wolf kept straight on to the shallows, crossed them, Boru beside her, then followed the water in its downstream course to where it curved in a broad bend with willows clothing both borders and growing out into the current. Here, with a side glance at Boru, she crouched and lay with quick-panting sides, striving to regain normal breathing. Following her example, Boru set himself beside her at the edge of the willows, hidden by the new foliage at the bend of the U formed by the curve of the river, both watching the margin of the stream below them where it gathered itself into riffles, murmuring faintly as the stones fought the contracting current.

The stars grew fainter and the sky grayer as they kept vigil with nose and eye and ear, listening to the hidden rustlings on the hill mounting to the first ridge. The sky commenced to quiver, the outlines of the distant hills began to show clearly, and a rim of rose streaked the higher peaks, broadening as it descended.

A twig cracked, the she-wolf sank her head between her forepaws, her ears sharp-angled, her haunches twitching with excitement. Boru, tensely eager, strained his vision downstream.

A buck, eight-pointed, his horns in the spring velvet, his coat glossy, and his body plump, stepped noiselessly from the thicket into the shallows and surveyed the prospect. His head was proudly erect; his broad, moist nostrils opened and contracted, while his great, lustrous eyes suspiciously swept upstream and down. So silently did he step, so suddenly did he take shape in the dim dawnlight that Boru blinked his eyes, believing that he had been caught napping. The she-wolf turned her head ever so slightly with a silent grin of warning, and Boru, quivering with restraint, waited for her to take the lead.

What little wind there was blew from the buck to the wolves. Finally, with gathering courage, he waded in deeper, until the stream ran above his fetlocks, and commenced to drink. At this assurance of safety, two does stepped daintily out of the willows and started to follow his example. The she-wolf rose as silently as if she had been a shadow and crept forward stealthily, foot by foot. Boru, less expert and heavier, stepped upon a twig that cracked sharply in the quiet dawn. He caught one swift glance of reproach from his mate's eye, and the next second he was leading her, eager to retrieve his mistake, as they charged at top speed out of the willows.

The sound of the breaking twig appeared to petrify the deer for the fraction of a second, and they stood like statues, the water dripping from their muzzles, their heads up, and their large ears erect. Then the does broke for cover, reaching the willows as Boru and the she-wolf splashed into the water in an attempt to cut out the buck.

Boru, his action impeded by the flow of the current, found

himself in danger. He had not thought of the deer showing fight, but the buck, with lowered antlers, threatened
with vigorous side sweeps to impale him. Boru did not
know that the velvet-covered horns with their soft cores
were not the dangerous weapons they appeared or would
be in the course of a few weeks. The she-wolf knew better, but she also declined the risk and snapped and snarled
at the buck's gambrels. The buck struck out with his hind
quarters, and the wolf dodged; while Boru, baying in his
excitement, strove to get past the fence of antlers and reach
the throat of the deer. The wolf worked silently, a lesson
of the wild to avoid interference and a possible fight for
the quarry that was in the long list of things Boru had yet
to learn. The buck whirled nimbly, attempting with chisel-
edged hoofs and with his tender horns to cripple his adver-
saries. The water was thrashed into a foamy turmoil, the
trout fled the riffles as the does, with the fawns they had
left hidden in the thicket, went crashing up the ridge to
safety, pausing at length on a high bench to look down at
the combat with great, frightened eyes.

The buck was fearful of the deeper water which would
leave his outstretched throat defenceless, and he was afraid
of the shore; but at last he decided to trust to his best ally,
his speed, and, with a final, savage kick at the she-wolf,
and a raking toss that caught Boru under the shoulder and

tumbled him asprawl in the shallows, made for the beach. The top line of his right antler broke off, leaving the horn raw and bleeding, and Boru, unwounded and recovering his feet, dashed after him, getting between him and the trees. The buck wheeled and galloped down the sand strip, the grit flying from his hoofs.

Boru saw his mate come in from the water, a white streak of speed striking at the buck's hocks. Free of the water, her first snap severed the gambrel joint and the buck staggered. Two more swift scissor strokes of her fangs, and the deer's hind legs were useless, leaving him to stand, crippled, on his gambrels instead of his hind feet. He raised his head in tortured protest, and Boru sprang for the throat, tearing through windpipe and jugular at one slash of his tusks, backed by the impulse and the weight of his body.

The buck sank to the sand, dyeing it with his blood, as the sun, rising above Tamarack Flat, reddened all the hills with sudden splendor, while Boru and his mate devoured their first kill, gorging themselves to satiety over their self-provided wedding feast.

The den was a low-fronted hole in the face of a ledge of rocks, high up in the hills, overlooking a lonely mountain tarn, whose water reflected the perpetual snow of the pyramidal peak that dominated the range. In front of the cave

OFTEN HIS MATE LAY OUT IN THE SUNSHINE SUCKLING HER
DARLINGS, OR TEACHING THEM SUCH TRICKS AS THEIR BABY
BRAINS COULD COMPREHEND

there was a platform that seemed to have been made especially for the play of wolf whelps.

The top of the ledge was an ideal basking place for their parents. It was below timber line, tall hemlocks and hardwood trees grew close to the face of the cliffs, and the fallen leaves and needles had carpeted the place for ages. In the center of the rock on top of the ledge was a ring of dead leaves about six inches high, all worn to fine, soft shreds and mingled with coarse gray hair. This was Boru's day bed, where he would lie for hours looking over the lake and the summits of the hills, or watching his cubs at play on the platform below. Often his mate lay out in the sunshine suckling her seven darlings, or teaching them such tricks as their baby brains could comprehend, coaxing them to snap and snarl at each other and acquire self-defense, rolling their furry bodies over on their backs with her muzzle to show them where to strike when their teeth grew long and strong enough.

Boru felt a glow of pride whenever he looked at his offspring, coupled with a sense of grave responsibility. The whelps were four weeks old now. Boru had known freedom for thirteen weeks, during which time he had barely thought of man and had kept aloof from sight or scent of him. He had learned a lot of woodcraft in the past three months. Much of it had come to him as the revival of half-

forgotten memories, much of it he owed to his mate. Without her he would have gone hungry many a time, though
food was plentiful. In the first weeks of their mating, she
had shown him how to work uphill and cut off the wood-
chucks from their holes; where to look for rabbits, grouse
and quail. Twice since their first buck they had killed
deer, lying in wait for them at a salt lick, hunting upwind
and making short work of the terrified does. He learned to
like many berries and the refreshingly acid tips of certain
shrubs that served at once as salad and corrective to their
meat diet. The two of them were afraid of nothing.
They were overlords of the wild. Once, at twilight, they
had come upon a panther outstretched upon the butt of a
fallen tree that reached over the lake close to the surface.
As Boru and his mate trotted noiselessly out of a tangle of
wild grapevine that curtained the birches and elder trees,
the panther, with a lightning thrust of one paw, sent a
plump lake trout flying from the water and scurrying along
the shore. Before the great cat, turning leisurely to retrieve his flapping capture, could reach it, Boru and the she-
wolf barred the way.

The panther crouched with flaming eyes, tip-twitching
tail, and ears flattened to its round skull, and launched itself furiously into the air, striking out with unsheathed
claws at the robbers. Boru and his mate dodged out as the

panther landed, then in, slashing swiftly with their tusks and retreating out of reach before the astounded panther, torn on either flank and shoulder, knew the attack was on. They harried him with lightning dashes at his hind quarters, one darting in as the panther whirled to rend the other elusive adversary, until his tawny hide showed bars of scarlet. It did not take much of this sort of fighting to cause the loss of the panther's appetite for fish, and, with one last coughing snarl of defiance, he made for the trees. Boru followed him to the edge of the woods, where the panther took to the boughs, then returned at the warning yap of the she-wolf, who knew that their advantage lay in open ground. In the meantime, she had appropriated the trout which Boru had forgotten in the fast fury of the fight and the smart of a shallow but painful gash in his shoulder, where the panther's claws had raked him.

Once they had surprised a bear, gruntingly content over the carcass of a fawn and, at the she-wolf's signal, they had charged upon his flanks. Bruin had risen on his hind quarters, quickly estimated the weight and valor of his foes, and then, with his little eyes inflamed with rage, lumbered off, having had earlier experience with wolves that made him wary. There was practically nothing left of the fawn, but it was good sport driving off the burly butcher, and they laughed together over the fun and excitement of it.

Boru's first primitive passion that had overmastered him when he mated had turned to a deep emotion founded upon his respect for the she-wolf's courage and wisdom, strengthened by the beauty she held in his eyes. And each day intensified his feeling. It was a wonderful life, a constant revelation to Boru, whose activities had been hitherto limited to a theatrical performance. Days they nested in a favorite thicket, rousing at dusk to roam free until the next day's sun grew hot, sometimes lying in wait for a deer by licks and runways, foraging for rabbits, grouse and quail, or circumventing woodchucks.

At the end of the second month, when his mate was heavy with her motherhood, Boru did most of the hunting, making his kill and bringing her share to his mate. As the whelping time came closer, they hunted for a den, and, to his pride, it was Boru who came across the home overlooking the lake and received the approval of his lady for the wisdom of his choice. And there the wolflings were born.

Curious little blind lumps Boru thought them as they whiningly crawled motherward in the first dark days of their infancy; and later he wondered if they were ever going to be able to run and leap and fight, so long, so loosely jointed and generally wabbly they seemed. They were all very dark of coat except one female, who was white except for a gray saddle patch on the right side and one gray ear. Her eyes, as they changed from the first uncertain hues of puppydom, were greenish amber, like the mother's; the rest's were dark, like Boru's, and three of them had collie ears, like their father.

Boru never played with them, though he was sometimes tempted to do so with his favorite, the little white bitch. But the mother resented any interference with her training, and Boru found it best to maintain a dignified watch while his mate gradually and lovingly expounded the education of a wolf whelp.

He did not altogether understand her methods in the beginning. He could not understand why she wanted to leave the cubs hidden in the den and go hunting. He was perfectly capable of that for all hands, he considered, until he began to realize that a continuous stay in the den was neither interesting nor healthy for the mother, and to comprehend that his mate, for all her ardent and evident admiration of him, had a decided mind of her own. So they shared the duty of providing food for the family, making their kill and hurrying straight back to the den to disgorge a meal for the cubs.

It was an idyl of the wild made up of the joy of strength and freedom, the delight of ardent loving and the pride of reproducing their kind.

Boru, as he lay basking in the early sun, was rarely troubled with remembrances of the days before his flight.   He was too content to reason.   It seemed as if he had always belonged here in the mountains, with his mate lying luxuriously relaxed on the platform beneath him, blinking as her whelps nuzzled closer to her breasts, rolling one eye affectionately upward once in a while to gaze at him. There were no sights or sounds or scents in the wilderness to urge the storage cells of his brain to reminiscence.   He looked back at his man-mastered life through a veil of fear and dislike.   The one memory that had once most persistently recurred, the vision of a woman who had petted him and whom he had been gladly eager to serve, never came back during these days.

A shadow drifted over him, and he looked up lazily. Far above, an eagle soared.   He had noticed the great bird two or three times before.   It seemed to have its aerie by the pyramidal peak, and he had seen it sweep down, a swiftly moving speck against the snow, and go scouting on proud wings, disdainful of fur-coated things that could not leave the ground.

As he watched, the bird descended in a long spiral, glided up again, breasting an air wave, and in perfect volitation dipped beyond the summit of a ridge.

Boru stretched, yawned, and stretched again, licked his

chops in pleasant memory of last night's woodchuck, dropped softly on his pads to the little platform, nipped his mate lovingly on one ear, and went into the den to sleep. Presently, the greediness of her youngsters abated, his mate followed, driving in the whelps ahead of her. A little later, the sunny ledge was once more darkened by a passing shadow as the eagle, ranging the airways, soared again above the lake and then, as if disappointed, swept on in search of more promising larders.

While Boru was a devoted mate and father, there were times when, his duties as provider filled, he wandered off on enterprises of his own. There was still much that was fascinatingly strange to him in his new surroundings, and he was keen to explore every promising avenue of adventure. Several times he had heard the ululating chorus of the wolf pack that ranged the hills near the den, but he felt no wish to join them. His love for his mate did not overcome his hereditary hatred of all her breed, and the she-wolf had no desire to mingle with her kind who had estranged her on account of her conspicuous color. But one night, his stomach contented soon after midnight with a coon that had ventured up from his usual haunts in the lower valleys for a bacchanal revel on wild grapes, Boru, ambling denward by moonlight, heard the solo of the leader of the pack from the bottom of the gulch that lay between him and the home ridge.

Though it was not the call of his own clan, this bugle summons of the night always started Boru's hair to lifting, brought an ecstatic gush of moisture from his salivary glands, and roused within him a wild desire to race with a pack of his own, outtiring the deer that bounded away in frightened leaps before them, or better still, rushing on to do battle with his enemies.

He stole cautiously along the ridge in the shadow, taking care not to show himself, and, following upwind, found a projecting buttress of rock, dropped down to it, and, with his head set between his paws, peered down at the bottom of the ravine.

The gulch was strewn with bowlders, glacier-laid, with only a few stunted trees growing in scattered fashion. Below Boru squatted the wolf pack, in a ring, thirty-odd of them, their noses pointing inward to where the leader sat. He raised his muzzle to the sky, and the rest followed his example like a class at physical culture, or an orchestra waiting for the upbeat of the baton. The leader lifted his muzzle higher, and from between his curled-back lips issued a sobbing wail, tenor in quality, that sent waves of resentment over Boru's spirit. The pack caught the pitch and swelled the throbbing anguish of the chorus. The howling ceased simultaneously, and there was a short interval until the leader once more started the chant.

The wolves were in Boru's direct trail home. He was in no mood to make a long circuit, and he was not rash enough to attempt to pass in sight of the pack, which would probably attack him. And, aside from his enmity, the sensations aroused by the chorus held a certain distinct quality of pleasure. Perched above them, he patiently waited the end of the performance. Whatever its inspiration, it was not the prelude to a hunt, for the wild choristers kept it up until the sky grayed before they trotted to the head of the gulch, stopped suspiciously to sniff as they passed to leeward of Boru and caught his scent, then, warned by the increasing light, loped up the ravine and disappeared among the trees.

Boru crossed the gulch and climbed the ridge that formed part of the basin of the lake. High up, he saw the eagle, and watched it drop like a plummet as it sighted its prey. Simultaneously he heard a sharp yap of his mate, followed by a howl that sounded pain and distress, a call for help. Boru broke into a gallop. The eagle had dropped close to the den, half a mile away along the ridge. Boru straightened out his long legs and leaped, bounding over bowlders, dodging through the hemlocks as he rushed to the aid of his mate.

As he reached the ledge above the cave, the great bird

rose heavily, flapping its great wings, bearing in its talons the white, limp burden of the whelp bitch, while the mother wolf howled in helpless rage.   Boru sprang to the platform as the eagle bore out across the lake.   It was a male bald-eagle, an old bird, with its tail feathers white, as well as those of head and neck.   Boru glimpsed its implacable eye as he jumped.   His mate, blinded by the blood that poured from a gash between the eyes where the bird's iron beak had struck home, gave him a swift whine of welcome. Some scattered feathers showed her attempt at defense.

The whelps, scared at the furious struggle that had swept the little platform, had retreated into the den, and now stood, whimpering, at the entrance, till they were joined by their mother and Boru.

All that day Boru licked the gash between the eyes of his mate, while she occasionally touched him with her tongue for thanks.   It healed within a day or two, but for a week she kept the cubs in the cave during daylight, and, by mutual consent, both of them never left them at the same time.

Probably if the cubs had all been the same color they would have forgotten their loss more readily, being unable to count; but they constantly missed the one white whelp of the litter, the only one with wolf eyes, and Boru brooded in hopes of revenge, lying in the cave mouth or in his nest on top of the ledge, watching for the eagle, hoping to get close enough to take toll for their misfortune.

He resented the eagle's challenge of his supremacy over what he had self-proclaimed as his domain, and pondered how he could attack this creature who could descend from unassailable heights to carry off their whelps with impunity to some place where none could follow.

Days passed, and the eagle failed to make an appearance above the lake. The memory of the bitch whelp faded, as the rest grew more lively and aggressive and the time grew near when, at ten weeks old, the family, according to wolf custom, would leave the den until the next spring and train the cubs to night hunting.

One night, the she-wolf was forced to travel far for her kill, and had not returned to the den as usual by daybreak. As the sun, rising behind the shoulder of the great peak, struck the ledge, Boru emerged from the cave and stretched himself, yawning vigorously in the crisp morning air. After him tumbled the cubs, gaping in imitation of their father's actions and settling down to rough-and-tumble play among themselves.

Boru, watched them for a while, cuffing three of them away when they simultaneously attacked a fourth too vigorously. Then he jumped easily up the projections of the ledge to his nest on top, circled about until he found the right angle of comfort, and dropped contentedly in his lair of leaves.   Closing his eyes before the level rays of the sun, drowsiness soon overtook him, and he slept soundly.

He was aroused by yelps from the cubs and a downward rush of wind that vigorously ruffled his fur.   He awoke to see the form of the eagle with wide-spread wings between him and the sun, swooping to the platform, hungry for fresh whelp meat.   It was twenty feet to where the cubs cowered, and Boru, with a roar, took it at a leap, reaching the platform as the eagle, beak agape and talons distended, his great pinions and the rudder of his tail arresting his drop, landed, striking Boru, unbalanced from his leap, and rolling him over with the force of the impact.   Boru felt the sharp talons gripping him by the lower ribs, close to his unprotected belly, and bit savagely upward at the body of the eagle, thick-mailed with feathers.   His mouth closed on plumage at each snapping slash, and he tried to regain his feet, but the weight of the bird, beating him back with its mighty pinions, confused him.

He saw the powerful beak, poised between the relentless eyes driving at him, and twisted his head to one side.   The blow hit him on the neck just below the jaw with stunning force, striking straight at the jugular.

Once more, as it had in his first wolf fight, the emblem of his former servitude—his collar—saved him.   The

wolf's fang had scored the leather, but Boru had been unable to rid himself of it, had, indeed, accepted it as part
and parcel of his natural equipment. The eagle's beak
struck the heavy brass studding and glanced aside, tearing
through the stiff leather and striking the rock harmlessly.

Boru snapped at the bird's neck, but the stiff-quilled
feathers baffled him. Squirming desperately as the eagle
raised its head for another hammer stroke, he curved his
spine to a bow and slashed once more. This time his teeth
sank through the softer feathers of the breast, and swiftly
chiseled their way through warm, yielding flesh. The
eagle's plumage was quickly stained with blood, and it
screamed with pain and surprise. The taste of the blood
was sweet in Boru's mouth, and, as the baffled bird stabbed
at him, he made a sidelong bite that caught the eagle's scaly
leg just above the spur fairly in the vise of his back teeth.
He crunched as the eagle's beak scored his shoulder, and
his powerful jaws sheared through gristle, bone and sinew.

The bird screamed again, the hollows of his wings held
the air and, driving with all his force, inspired by terror,
he rose slowly from the platform. Boru's last scissors snap
dragged free two of the big tail feathers. He rolled swiftly
to his feet and barked defiance at the defeated sky raider,
rising in circles with frantic speed. The eagle was not
mortally wounded, but he was badly mained and crestfallen.

He had learned a lesson—to let wolf whelps most severely alone.

Boru watched his flight in anticipation of a possible return, then took stock of the outcome of the fight. The wound on his shoulder was not a bad one—and he licked it philosophically, counting the victory well worth the cost. There was blood on the rock, some of it his, some of it the eagle's, and he lapped it up impartially.

When the she-wolf, hearing the eagle's scream, came galloping up in haste and alarm, she found Boru licking his wound, stopping now and then to watch the antics of the cubs, who were playing with the severed talons.

The cubs were ten weeks old, and the time had come to take them from the den and teach them to range and kill. The den was to be deserted for another year until there was another litter of whelps to be given shelter during their first weeks of helplessness. After they had been tutored through one winter, the law of the wild provided that the young wolves should be led thirty or forty miles from their old home and taught that they were henceforth to trust to their own resources. But in the meantime their real education was to be accomplished.

Boru and his mate still hunted at will for the main larder, but every night they taught the youngsters to travel as far as their half-grown strength would permit, teaching them the habits of the creatures they preyed upon and the main factors of the hunting code. Often one of them would kill close to the day-time haunt so that the cubs could worry the carcass. Sometimes they rounded up a covey of grouse or quail, the cubs lying hidden in the brush, their bright eyes watching every move; and then, the birds huddled, hie on the whelps to the slaughter. Or they would take them to the lower hills, where the rock rabbits lived, and show them how to hunt in couples, one heading off the squealing bunny while the other cracked its spine at a snap.

Fights between them were encouraged, with Boru and his mate as arbiters, the latter stopping the combat when it threatened to become dangerous, or cuffing on a weak-spirited cub to face the foe.

By day they nested in the brush, the cubs woven together in a warm bundle, Boru and the she-wolf close to each other, usually flat on their sides, with their noses touching. Their nests were carefully chosen and securely hidden, but their chief security was their supremacy as a fighting combination. Now that the eagle had been driven off, they were once more the masters of the hills they roamed. Only the members of the wolf pack could have conquered them, and by them they were left alone. Boru's great size, and the knowledge of his prowess, which was the gossip of the hills, had a good deal to do with securing this immunity.

He was now in perfect condition of wind and limb, with sinews and muscles as hard as steel, the machine absolute, capable of ranging fifty miles at night without thought of fatigue, the fighting peer of anything that wore claws.

One moon, after a hard night's travel, Boru's mate aroused him by whining as she stood wakeful and restless beside him. He jumped up to join her as she sniffed the air uneasily, shifting her sensitive muzzle to all quarters. There was practically no wind, and it was intensely hot. A faint mist seemed rising with a peculiar, pungent smell that was almost stifling.

The cubs were told to stay quiet, and the she-wolf led the way from the cover, trotting with Boru to a rocky point at the ridge summit. They had made their hunting grounds and training quarters for the cubs on another side of the great, pyramidal peak from that which sheltered the lake. From the mountain two main spurs stretched in a great V, filled with minor gulches. On the ridge where they stood, between two of these lesser ravines, they noted great clouds of the same blue-gray mist, shot here and there with red tongues the color of sunset fires. A crackling sound came to them, menacing, steadily growing nearer and louder.

To their right, from a cleft in the spur called Windy Gap, where on the stillest day the wind blew strongly, the

BORU FELT THE SHARP TALONS GRIPPING HIM BY THE RIBS AND
BIT SAVAGELY UPWARD AT THE BODY OF THE EAGLE

red tongues grew brighter, licking greedily down one of
the smoke-veiled ridges. Grouse and quail whirred by below them, smaller birds were flying above their heads, chat-
tering as they went. They could hear the brush crack as
animals broke through it at top speed. In the few seconds
they gazed, three deer, bounding leap for leap with a
panther, their sides laboring, crashed close to them through
the thicket. They caught the infection of fear. The forest was on fire.

The smoke clouds, flecked with flying brands, closed in
on all sides. The heat was momentarily growing worse,
and the crackling had turned into a roar. In flight lay the
only escape, and in the uncertainty of the direction of the
flames the only sure safety lay on the barren slopes of the
mountain.

To gain that, they had three ridges to cross, all smoke-
wreathed, all threatening to burst into open conflagration.

The cubs, whining at the heat and smoke, were hunted
from the cover and ordered to follow. They galloped at
top speed to the ridge behind Boru and their mother; then
down into the gulch, where all lapped thirstily at the water
of a little creek already warm and scummed with wood ash.
Up again through the stinging, blinding smoke they fought,
Boru and his mate urging on the cubs with pushes and bites,
driving them to the mountain.

As they topped the next ridge, a tongue of flame ran along the ferns, a puff of wind blew the smoke aside and showed the fire roaring toward them amid the trees.   They leaped the burning fern and fled down once more with only two ridges between them and safety on the granite of the peak at the apex of the spurs.

Only three cubs were left of the six when the next ridge was crossed, and they could barely move.   Boru's eyes were scalded, his lungs a furnace, and breathing a torture, his coat was scorched, and here and there a flying torch had burned through to the flesh.   His mate was in no better case, and the cubs were on the point of exhaustion.   Half-way down the slope, another fell behind.   Boru and the she-wolf were too blind to notice anything but that there were still cubs with them, and they nosed them on.   There was another stream here, and they blundered mercifully into a pool that was still fairly cool.   It stung their burns, but it relieved them and gave them a little fresh energy for the final scramble.

The last climb was a steep one.   The cub in front of Boru sank utterly exhausted, unable to move.   Behind them the gulch was filled with smoke reddened in great patches by the flames.   Boru tried in vain to rouse the cub to another effort.   He gripped the loose skin of its neck in an attempt to carry or at least drag it along, but his own strength was failing rapidly. His mate had gone on with the other cub, the last of the litter.

Reluctantly he left the now unconscious cub, and followed its mother up the hill. As long as she was safe, he cared little. The saving of his offspring was instinct; his feeling for her something deeper, stronger, more impelling. Close to the summit, he found her coming back. She had missed the surviving cub in the smoke, and was looking for it. Boru whined to her, but she passed him with a little sound of protest, her tortured nose trying to find some trace of her offspring. The breeze broke through the smoke again and showed the bare granite of the mountains, where there was nothing to feed the fire; and, beyond, a vision of delight, the white snow beds that crested the mountain. It seemed to Boru the wind was laden with their cool breath; a few more leaps and the day was won.

He looked back to where the white form of his mate showed dimly as she limped painfully through the smoke, urged by her mother love to find the cub Boru knew was hopelessly lost.

For a second he wavered. Above him the smoke was closing in on the snowy panorama of the peak. Below the rolling clouds were dyed red by the oncoming flames. Into the danger his mate had disappeared. Up to safety he would not climb alone. He turned his scorched head downhill and gave a choking bark from his parched throat.   It was his message to his mate, his pledge of fealty.

Instinct urged him to self preservation—the first law of Nature.   Equally something moved deep-set within him that urged him to achieve the rescue of his love or perish with her.   This was a development emerging from his maturity, motivated by the memory of the joyous hours spent together.

The two conflicted.   Desperate as the moment was, infinitely brief respite that he was granted, he had to achieve decision, create thought.   He made selection.   And again he sent his pledge of fealty to his mate.

CHAPTER THREE

DESOLATION

In a deep cañon close to where the naked granite of the pyramidal peak that topped the range halted the upward march of the forest, a stream, fed by the perpetual snow fields, ran deep and strong between steep walls once covered with ferns and underbrush, now smudged and barren. Close to the water's edge showed the low-roofed opening of a cave. The tunnel ran far back into the cliff, grading downward for over a hundred feet to an inner chamber.

Stretched out side by side, close to the farther wall, lay Boru and his mate, unconscious, half suffocated, but alive. Caught in the fire that had ravaged the range from river edge to timber line, the wolf bitch had turned back on the verge of safety to rescue the last of her whelps that had passed the peril of smoke and flame. Boru, following her, had reached her as, maddened with the heat, she had plunged into the stream, her cub tight gripped between her teeth. A pitying puff of wind had swept aside the eddying smoke that filled the gorge long enough for Boru to sight the mouth of the cave and guide her to the refuge.

Above, where the trees were thick, the fire raged hotly, but at the cave end Boru and his mate found comparative coolness and sufficient air to preserve life, if not their senses. The night wind, cool from the snow fields, cleared the gorge while the lower forests burned themselves out, and the two lay prone, hardly breathing, far into the next afternoon.

Boru recovered first, slowly regaining consciousness, but too exhausted to move or realize his surroundings. His thick gray coat was scorched, patches of it had rubbed off, and the unprotected flesh beneath was raw. His eyes, seared and bloodshot, throbbed as he tried to pierce the gloom of the cavern. His throat was a torment, and his parched tongue, dry and swollen, protruded from his jaws. The raising of his head was an agony, and he dropped it again in pain and weakness. His muzzle in its new position struck the shaggy fur of his mate, and recollection returned swiftly. With it was the thought of the water outside, and he staggered to his legs, whining at the pain that racked him.

The cub lay dead at his feet. He nosed it for a second, then bent his head above his mate's and nuzzled her. She whimpered, smelled him, and tried to rise, succeeding painfully at last. Her eyes, better than those of her wolf-hound mate for darkness, spied her whelp. She tried to lick it back to life with her cracked tongue, but soon recog-

nized the uselessness of trying to revive the stiffened body.
She, too, remembered the water, and her scent placed it.
Totteringly she led the way, and Boru followed, toiling
forward on legs that barely supported them.

The way was steep as they scrambled on, burning with
thirst and the fever of their burns. Suddenly the wolf
bitch stopped, went on for a few steps, and howled. Boru
recognized the note of fear and passed her. Earth was
banked high in front of them. As he mounted it his back
struck the cave roof. The way to water and liberty was
barred! The roof of the tunnel had fallen in and made
them prisoners, wounded, faint from fatigue and hunger,
dying for water to replace the moisture that the heat had
sucked from their bodies in their struggle through the fire.

Boru felt his mate's body pitch suddenly forward as her
legs failed her in her despair, and he gave her a whine of
encouragement. He nosed the roof, the landslide that
seemed to shut off all hope, and then the walls. Suddenly,
he touched moisture. The tumbling earth had diverted
the course of some deep-seated spring, and the water was
slowly forming on the side of the cavern over a face of rock.
Eagerly he lapped it. It was only a tiny trickle, but the
relief was exquisite. He lowered his head and touched his
wet nose to his mate's scorched muzzle. The contact
roused her, and she summoned her failing strength to raise

herself, crouching on her haunches, and, with sniffing ecstasy, to find the life-saving drip. Together they lapped the precious globules as they slowly formed, and with returning vitality hope revived. The cave-in was of loose soil and rock fragments, some air came through crevices they could not see, but that their remoistened nostrils sensed.

Boru scraped at the dirt. His pads were scorched and tender, but the earth gave way, and he persevered, sending the soil back of him in a steady shower as he burrowed. Side by side with him the she-wolf strove with laboring lungs. In their weakened condition, neither could work for long, and every few minutes they rested, the sweat slavering from their tongues, licking the wet surface of the rock and waiting to get their lungs under control before they once more desperately attacked their heartbreaking task.

Twice the earth shifted and fell as they rapidly backed out. Once it nearly smothered Boru before he could scramble clear, but they returned to the toil with undaunted persistency. The third time the dirt settled into the burrows they had dug, and left a clear space at the top. At this they sprang with frantic endeavor, whining as they struggled. Boru broke through at last, with his mate at his heels, and made shift to achieve a broken lope for the mouth of the cave.

Down the slope, they tumbled together into the stream, open-mouthed, and swam in the cool water, ignoring the smart of its contact with their wounds in the sheer delight of its flowing over parched gums and tongues and palates.

A charred tree stump lay half submerged. Against it the bodies of half a dozen plump trout, killed by the heat, had drifted. These they seized and bolted on the bank, then lay down side by side on a narrow strip of shingle to rest and take stock of their injuries.

Boru's eyes hurt horribly, his whole coat was singed, and the raw scalds on his sides made it impossible for him to find a tolerable position on the gravel. His mate was in equally evil case. Her muzzle showed red where the heat had cracked it, one paw was badly burned, and the magnificent plume of her brush was reduced to a frazzle length of sparsely furred vertebræ. Boru's gray coat was smeared with charcoal and ashes, and his mate's white fur was pitifully stained. The sting of their burns kept them shifting uneasily as they licked the injured places and whimpered at their tenderness. Every little while they lapped the cold stream to allay a thirst that refused to be assuaged. Hunger still asserted itself, and presently they ranged the stream looking for more fish. They found a few stranded in the shallows and devoured them, then climbed the ridge, anxious to get clear of the desolation of the burned forest, once their well-stocked hunting ground.

On top of the ridge, limping silently across the rise over the ashes that covered the ground, they came upon five buzzards clustered about the carcass of a deer and charged the carrion eaters. The bloated birds flopped heavily and resentfully off and squatted on the ground a little distance away, croaking as they opened their blood-stained beaks in protest. There was little left of the impromptu barbecue except some of the larger bones. These Boru and the she-wolf crushed for the rich marrow. The meal ended, they stretched themselves out, resting before farther travel.

Boru's weary eyes blinked, and, stretching his head between his paws, he found oblivion in sleep. When he awoke the sun was low and the sky red between the scattered pines that were still burning. The she-wolf lay on her side, her legs wide-stretched, her ribs rising and falling as she breathed. Four of the buzzards roosted persistently on the limb of a gaunt tree, the blackened bark of which had split and shredded, showing the ghastly under skin; a specter of the forest. The fifth bird stood close beside him, eying him with hungry speculation. Boru sprang to his feet, and the buzzard ran off clumsily, spreading its pinions till they caught the air beneath the feathered planes, then rising into the air and soaring downhill, followed by its disappointed fellow gluttons.

The she-wolf rose, yawning. She lifted her head and shifted it from side to side, as if trying to get her bearings, snuffing the wind and glancing oftenest at the bare shoulder of the peak above them, beyond which a serene moon was slowly lifting.

Boru knew her ways and watched her, quietly awaiting her lead. She came to a decision at last and limped upward, apparently following an assured trail. Boru trotted beside her, both of them lame, their pads, as they reached the barrent granite, leaving little splotches of blood in their tracks.

The she-wolf held on determinedly, and Boru gave her the leadership, positive that she acted with full reason. They traveled for two hours, crossing the shoulder of the mountain in a direction opposite to that which he had himself thought vaguely of taking, in which lay the lake where they had made their den in the shore cliffs and reared their whelps.

Their wounds stiffened as the night grew cooler, but they forged grimly on. Two or three times the she-wolf turned and thrust her muzzle at Boru, and he controlled his panting and nipped back affectionately.

They crossed the peak at a tangent, and presently the night wind bore the balsam of green trees. There was healing in the tang, and Boru longed for the shade of verdant woods and the comfort of a yielding bed of pine needles. The she-wolf swung her head toward him, with her nose wrinkled in pleasure, and quickened her pace. They reached the first trees and plunged beneath their shadow, working down to the bottom of the ravine.

The gorge was a natural stone corridor running into the mountainside like a roofless tunnel, ending in sheer granite walls, impassable to anything but a mountain sheep. The cliffs sloped less abruptly where Boru and his mate lamely made their way to the bottom of the ravine.

An odor that was exquisite came to the she-wolf. She recognized the smell of sulphur and knew the healing qualities of the pool that revealed itself, surrounded by stones whitened by the deposit of the mineral, and beside which spouted the geyser in a basin of its own. It was a long time since she had visited it, but she had led the way unerringly, and now looked back with rolling eye and lolling tongue of triumph at Boru, jogging painfully over the stony floor.

As they came closer to the margin of the pool and could see more clearly through the veil of steamy mist, the she-wolf suddenly halted, the ruff lifted about her neck, and

IN THE CENTER LAY A BLACK MASS THAT BORU HAD TAKEN FOR A ROCK, THROUGH THE MIST. IT WAS A BROWN MOUNTAIN BEAR

the fur bristled along her spine while her gums curled back in a snarl. Boru caught up with her and instantly imitated her action. The pool was pre-empted.

In the center lay a black mass that Boru had taken for a rock through the mist. No warning odor had been able to penetrate the sulphurous air. But now closer sight revealed a pair of small eyes gleaming in the moonlight like crimson spangles on a fur robe. A piggish snout lay just above the surface of the water, moving from side to side as the eyes roved, uneasily watching the intruders. It was a brown mountain bear, not a cinnamon, but a formidable opponent, who was making his season's visit to the healing spring. He had only arrived an hour or two before, he was comfortable, he intended to stay for at least two or three days, and he resented the intrusion of the two gaunt, dilapidated creatures glaring and snarling at him from the bank.

He told them so in grunting protest, but waited for them to make the first move. They looked played out, he decided, as his cunning eyes appraised them. Possession was his, and they might not care to dispute it. He emphasized his reasoning with a deep growl.

Boru's nerves were already strained to the point where it took very little to short-circuit them. He was desperately tired, tortured with his wounds, and the growl of the bear was the last straw on the burden of his troubles. He charged to the attack with a roar of open-mouthed defiance, splashing recklessly through the spring straight for the bear, while his mate raced round the margin of the pool for a flank attack from the other side.

The bear raised himself angrily, swinging the swift club of his paw at Boru, who swerved as best he could in the water that reached to his lower ribs, and evaded the blow. The water hampered his fighting tactics, but he plunged forward to close combat, heedless in his inexperience of the power in the bear's forelegs and the lightninglike dexterity with which he could use them. To his amazement, as he sprang in and up to slash at the throat, the bear suddenly upreared on its hind quarters, towering above him, the great paws, with their rigid, tearing claws, ready for a rending smash.

At that moment the she-wolf's chisel teeth tore through fur and meat at the bear's flank, and at the shock of the attack he swung clumsily about, dropping once more on all fours to face his new opponent, forgetting Boru for the moment.

Boru followed the tactics of his mate and slashed the flank on his side. As the bear turned, the she-wolf repeated the maneuver. This time Boru deep-scored the shoulder, his teeth grating on the bone. The sluggish sulphur water was lashed to heavy suds as the fight went on in the steaming pool, until at last the baffled bear, worried at his inability to cope with his enemies, lumbered from the spring, bleeding freely where they had gouged him.

On dry land, he wheeled and stood upright, once more striking right and left at Boru and the wolf as they shuttled in and out elusively, never attacking twice from the same angle. The water no longer hindered their methods, and the harried bear finally turned tail and scuttled down the cañon, his grunt turned to a whimper of protest, hoping that his surrender of the pool would rescue him from the fiends that followed, ripping his flanks, biting at his hocks.

Boru and the wolf accepted the retreat as a recognition of victory. They trotted back side by side contentedly to the pool, waded into the soft velvet comfort of its waters, and crouched together in the center, only their heads above the level of the water, sniffing luxuriantly, rejoicing in the smooth feel of the sulphur-laden liquid against their burns, lapping it now and then or laving their mouths with wide-opened jaws.

They lived in the box cañon for three weeks, ranging the lower end for food, but always returning to the sulphur pool and spending long hours in the soft, warm water.

Both their pelts renewed glossily as their systems took up the sulphur, their cracked pads and muzzles mended, and their limbs grew more supple every day.

Their larder was well stocked. The lower cañon sheltered willow grouse and rabbits in greater numbers than usual, tenanted as it was by many who had escaped from the fire. There were woodchucks a-plenty and juicy berries for dessert. For a while deer made the place their harborage, until Boru and his mate killed a buck as it came to the sulphur pool to drink and lick the incrusted stones. Then the herd took alarm and sought safer grazing. Other animals came to the spring to drink and bathe in the first few days, but the word soon spread concerning the destroyers who had made their headquarters at the top of the gulch, and the pair were left undisturbed and well contented.

Boru was a master woodsman now. His mate had no tricks of hunting craft left to teach him. His was the greater strength and speed, but his admiration of her had fostered the chivalry of his spirit, and he never took advantage of his superiority. He delighted at the sight of her, her white fur restored, the bushy plume of her tail carried proudly, as she ran beside him or gamboled gracefully in the playtimes when they forgot their maturity and frollicked like unweaned cub and puppy.

Boru's memories of the vaudeville life when he formed

part of the Canine Circus were never disturbed these days.

He was a primitive beast, obeying the laws of necessity, first the filling of his stomach, next the inclinations of sex that kept him the faithful comrade of his mate and inspired him to protect her in time of need. His paternal promptings had passed with her maternal ones until the next spring should bring around the breeding season, and once more they would comply with the greatest law of all and multiply.

As the days passed the larder became more scantily supplied, not so much by reason of their own appetites as the dread of their presence in the little world of the cañon.

With the waning of the moon they resolved to travel. For the first time since they had established themselves in the gorge, they went supperless to bed. Everything edible seemed to have made a sudden and most thorough exodus. Only some skunks and porcupines, bold in their established immunity, mocked their hunger. The berries, though luscious, were far from satisfying. The night air was chilly on the mountain height, and they slept at night in a cozy corner of the rocks that basined the warm geyser, a steam-heated apartment of their own, where the intermittent gushing of the eruptive spring disturbed them not at all.

It was to be their last night in the cañon. With the first coming of dawn, they had determined to start afield.

The night was dark, and the stars above the steam veil that always filmed the upper gorge were obscured by clouds that had commenced to gather at sunset in dense formation that betokened a storm. Both slept uneasily, partly from hunger, partly from subconscious anticipation of their next day's adventuring.

A little while after midnight Boru sprang to his feet, his blood tingling, every sense fully awakened, the white wolf beside him, quivering with eagerness, her ears high-pricked, jaws agape, sniffing the wind. Boru felt the fur lifting along his spine as the wind brought sound and scent of coming excitement.

Something was racing up the cañon toward them, crashing wildly through the brush, something with hoof that clicked on rocks and the smaller stones scattered by head-long flight. The telltale scent of a frightened deer betrayed it to the eager pair, their senses quickened by their craving appetites.

The wind was uncertain, but blew only in their direction, up the chimney of the ravine. The deer, crazed by terror, bounded on, unconscious of the enemies ahead, mindful only of the certain death that had followed him for two hard hours, despite his frantic efforts to escape. Behind him, urging him to blindly desperate speed, came the bay of his pursuers, the hunting howl of the wolf pack, calling to each other as they relentlessly gained on their prey.

Boru and the she-wolf heard the cry of the pack in the distance, but their brains barely registered it, so eager were they for the meal that was coming to them, four-footed, self-served. Boru stole swiftly and silently to the cliff while his mate guarded the other side of the space between the pool and the cañon wall through which the deer must pass.

The frightened buck came clattering over the bowlders, head back and antlers low. From the geyser rocks and the base of the cliff two forms rushed out like shadows, closing swiftly in on the deer's quarters. With two swift strokes the she-wolf severed the gambrel tendons, and the maimed deer dropped to its hocks, staggered, and fell on both knees. Boru, in mid-leap, slashed its throat as cleanly as if it had been done with a huge pair of shears. The buck fell, groaning, on its side, barely conscious of its fate, so swiftly had it come upon him.

The wolf cry sounded louder as the pack swept up the cañon The deer had been killed at the end of the gulch. On three sides the cliffs rose sheer. The pack, their tongues lolling from their jaws with the speed of the chase, keen at the imminent kill, running in an irregular V, caught sight of the barrier cliffs and knew the chase was over, spurting, with fierce yelps, for the first share of the meat. The wind had ceased suddenly, the air was ominous with the coming storm, lightning flickered above the cliffs, and the first tattoo of the thunder sounded. The wolf pack simultaneously caught the smell of the fresh blood, then sighted Boru and his mate devouring the carcass of the deer they had hunted so far and hard. Furious at the theft of their endeavor, they swept on, ravening to regain their prey and punish the marauders.

Above the buck's carcass, Boru and his mate turned to meet them undaunted by the odds, while recognizing the peril that beset them. The white wolf bitch knew the pack for the one that had cast her out on account of her conspicuous color, and yapped defiance at the leaders. Boru felt the gallant spirits of his wolf-hunting ancestors surging through him, intensifying his hatred, strengthening his heart for the fight. He felt no fear, only the lust of worthwhile combat. He cast one quick glance at his mate close beside him, leaving just room enough for free play, their haunches set against the back wall of the cañon, and waited for the nearest foe to come within reach. A vivid glare of lightning lit up the cañon and revealed the onrushing pack with eyes aflame and long tusks glistening. The thunder crashed overhead, and a few heavy drops spattered on the rocks and hissed into the pools. The next instant Boru had seized the too-eager leader and torn the life from his mangled throat. His mate closed with another, and the battle was joined.

There was no retreat for Boru and his mate, had they thought of it. To attempt to break through the cordon was to court destruction. The dead buck formed a barrier in front of them over which the wolves were forced to leap and scramble, shouldering each other aside in their impetuous assault. It was a fight to the death—thirty against two—fifteen against one. But the attack could only be made from the front and side, and the very numbers of the pack put them at a disadvantage.

It was a tragedy of the wilderness fought in a fit setting amid the barren cliffs, the geyser hissing its steamy column upward, the thunder pealing above them, the blackness of the cañon dispelled at intervals by the intense glare of lightning. At the flash, Boru, grim and bloody-jawed, gashed on chest and shoulders, would see an opponent launching through the air and catch the reek of fetid breath from the slavering mouth. He fought silently with rip and crunch and tear, shouldering his foes aside by superior weight and driving in to slash. He could give no heed to his mate in his own strait, but he was conscious of her fighting desperately beside him.

Three wolves, two at their last gasp, one dying, lay in front of him. The last, in a final, furious snap, caught his pastern, and Boru crunched through the neck vertebræ as another wolf closed in and gripped his throat.   Once more, for the third time, the badge of his past servitude, the heavy leather collar with its brass studs, saved him, entangling the wolf's teeth before it ripped apart and fell at his feet. With a snaky twist, Boru curved his neck and sank his teeth back of the wolf's windpipe, slitting the jugular vein. The wolf, with a last gurgle of hate, rolled over, hot blood spurting over its conqueror's fur.

There was no respite.   The white she-wolf had disposed of two of her opponents, but her white coat showed where their teeth had found her flesh.   The pack, maddened by resistance, surged in, the leaders snarling as they closed, the rear ranks howling their malice.   Giant as he was compared to the wolves, Boru could not hope long to withstand the odds.   The pack was attacking from the sides now, scrambling over each other to get at him.

The sheer weight of them would soon overpower him. But he fought on, his mouth filled with the blood of his enemies, his own dripping from his rough coat, his mane crested, his eyes blazing, and his spirit dauntless, though heart and lungs were laboring desperately to serve the calls upon them.

Suddenly his mate lurched against him, bewildered by a

sudden flank attack.   She slipped, fell on her side, and lay for the moment panting and defenseless.

A howl went up from the triumphing pack.   A blue sheet of flame with jagged forks of fire in the midst of it bathed the cañon in swift brilliance.   For the first time Boru gave tongue.   His roaring challenge sounded above the snarl of the pack, and he whirled to stand across the prostrate body of his mate as the wolves jumped in to end it.

Sudden darkness came as the lightning vanished, and a reverberating peal of thunder boomed and crashed until it seemed as if the cliffs were split apart.   The sky opened, and tons of water descended at the head of the gorge.   In an instant waterfalls were spouting over the edge of the cliffs, and the bed of the ravine was a raging torrent.   Boru, his mate, the dead wolves, and the living pack were swept away by the resistless fury of the cloudburst.   The ever-mounting wall of water surged between the cliffs, shifting great bowlders, plunging them against trees, uprooting pine and tamarack, and using them as rams to batter down others, swirling on to find an outlet, turbid, angry, resistless.

The next flash that split the inky pall showed trees tossing on the surface, their tops thrust upward as they ground over obstructions, the rain hammering hard upon the blunted waves, the cliffs caving in with sullen splash dulled by the noise of the downpour. Here and there, tossed like chips in a rapid, the buffeted forms of wolves swam vainly for refuge, half the pack already drowned or crushed against tree or rock.

Boru, after the first dazed moments of helplessness, found himself swimming strongly in the darkness, his chest high out of the water that raged around him, playing with him, mocking his endeavors to find a landing. The steady, pounding roar of the storm deafened him, the swift flashes of lightning revealed nothing but an eddying waste of water, foaming as it swept by. A tree bumped into him, submerging him, then another. Half choked, he paddled on. The next flash showed a pine ahead of him, its branches trailing its trunk and roots half awash. He fought hard to reach it as the darkness shut down, scrambling and slipping amid the tangle of boughs, caught in them one moment as in a net, struggling free the next, striving with momentary footholds to reach the trunk. The lower branches caught for an instant in something below the surface, dragged for a few seconds, then held the trunk steady as with an anchor while the tide rolled by.

Boru reached the great bole at last and ran swiftly along to its base, finding plenty of room where the trunk broadened at the roots.

As he stood there on trembling legs, exhausted, soaked to limpness, he heard a howl through the clamor of the storm and recognized his mate's cry of distress. He howled loudly in response. The cliffs seemed to leap from the night as the lightning flared. Twenty feet way, her eyes level with the water, battling hard for life, he saw the white she-wolf. She turned her head toward him, opened her jaws for a last piteous whine, and disappeared as the black curtain of the sky descended.

Gathering his uncertain legs beneath him, Boru leaped unhesitatingly into the water. In the dive he found her, clenching his teeth in the fur of her neck, striking out despairingly. A surge lifted them to the surface, an eddy tossed them by a freak of fate to where Boru could set his paws upon the roots of the tree still mercifully holding fast to the bottom. He dragged the she-wolf's head above the water, and she gasped; then, realizing her last hope of safety, found a submerged root with her hind feet. Too weak for further struggle, they rested for a few seconds, until with a final, frantic effort, they scrambled free of the water and lay across the trunk, exhausted.

The big pine shuddered, turned slightly, righted itself, the branches tore free, and, with the reunited couple clinging behind the buttress of its roots, plunged ahead, borne on by the clutching waves.

Dawn found them bedraggled, motionless, prone on their friendly raft, stranded by the spreading waters clear of the cañon in the middle of a glacial meadow set with great rounded bowlders.

The sky was clear as the rising sun stained the rim of the cliffs that walled the valley with a ribbon of rose that spread downward until the place was filled with golden light. Boru felt the kindly warmth and opened weary eyes. With an effort he lifted his head and licked the muzzle of his mate.

The summer came to an end, the trees clad themselves in their autumn dress as the days grew shorter and the air sharper. Only the evergreens remained unchanged. The first frost came and painted the aspens scarlet and the birches gold, then, tiring of the pastime, snapped the leaves from the twigs for a brief earth mantle. The fern bronzed and the underbrush shrank to bare branches. The wood-chucks holed up for the winter as the migrating birds left for the South and the arriving ducks and geese sought the lakes and rivers, telling of the winter that was following them.

Boru and his mate had returned to the den above the lake where they had reared their young. They had roamed the range and found no better place. Below them, to the east, lay the blackened area of their old hunting grounds destroyed by the fire. To the west, the untouched forest reached down to the river that bordered Tamarack Flat, far beneath them.

In the lower valleys were ranches, headquarters of the stock ranges that supplied the lumber district. Boru sometimes looked down on these from a ridge, noting the lazy smoke curling from the farm buildings by day, or watching the lighted windows at night, but he never went near them, knowing them for the abode of the beings he had foresworn and who had turned against him. It made him restless, and filled him with uneasiness mixed with a dim attraction that often brought him to lie, head on out-stretched paws, watching with his luminous, deep-brown eyes while the she-wolf lay beside him wondering at his abstraction, trotting off at last. Then Boru would follow, shaking off his mood as they struck trail or scent that prom-ised adventure or a meal.

Food grew scarce as the first snows fell. The few deer left since the fire vanished overnight; the rabbits kept close to their burrows, and the grouse, now that the underbrush was stripped, seemed always out of reach in the boughs. The winter had destroyed the cover for stealthy approaches, and the snow showed Boru's great bulk too plainly. His mate's white coat made her the more successful hunter, but as the heavier snows fell they often felt the pinch of empty bellies.

It was the third day since they had shared a too-confident mallard that the she-wolf had pounced upon in the sedge that bordered the lake. At nightfall they wandered far down the hillside, hoping to come across some unwary rabbit that one could cut off from shelter while the other ran it down.

There was no moon, but the star-shine and the snow made a comparative twilight through which they traveled lower than they had ever ventured. At the head of a valley they halted, looking across the snow. The sidehills were bare of trees save for a little orchard on the southern slope. A window showed a square of orange from a clump of trees surrounding a farmhouse. By some outbuildings two haystacks stood by a corral in which showed a huddle of dark objects. The wolf knew them as silly things covered with long, shaggy wool and protected by men and dogs, unable to bite or protect themselves—and very good to eat. She had tasted them once the winter before she was driven from the pack. She had made a foray with her little brother, and they had killed two of the helpless things one night and tried to once again after that, but dogs had barked furiously, a man had come hurrying up the hill and, as they were not particularly hungry that winter, they had decided the game not worth the risk.

But now she was ravenous. As her keen nose caught the scent, she licked her chops in a manner instantly understood by Boru and led the way along the ridge toward the ranch house.

Boru followed, a little disturbed at his near approach to the light that stood to him as a symbol of man's presence, but led on by his mate's unmistakable signs of a meal in close prospect. She halted on the ridge above the buildings and started down through the little orchard, Boru close behind. The sheep, in a corner of the inclosure, paid no attention to the danger prowling down upon them. The breeze blew uphill, and the rank muttony smell set Boru quivering with hungry impatience. Then a dog barked sharply, and the wolf flattened herself on the ground, indistinguishable against the snow. Boru crouched beside her instinctively. But his brain harbored a riot of emotions started by the once familiar sound of the hound's bark. It came again, and he started to reply. His mate heard the rumble beginning in his throat and turned her head, with a low snarl. Boru, ashamed, yet still not master of himself, choked back his answer.

Another oblong of light showed as a door opened and a man's voice called to the dog. Boru started to his feet.

There was something in the tone, aside from the humanity of it, that gripped at his heart. Memory stirred in his brain. He whined without knowing it, and his mate, angry at his stupidity, nipped him. The door closed, the light disappeared, and the dog did not bark again. Roused by his mate's wrath, Boru shook off the feeling of loneliness that had crept upon him with a desire to leave the she-wolf and go to the owner of the voice that had moved him so strangely. The muttony smell came more strongly, and his empty stomach clamored.

They crept through the orchard, and, hidden by the branching willows, followed the course of a little stream until they reached the haystacks.

In a few quick leaps they reached the corral fence. The bars were too close for them to pass easily. The sheep, aroused at last, blatted fearfully. The pitiful helplessness of the sound maddened Boru. Hunger-driven, he rose in a great leap, clearing the top rail easily, and rushed upon the frightened huddle. The she-wolf was beside him, and in a trice two ewes were kicking in their death flurry while the starving pair lapped their blood, drunk with the salty savor of it, feeling strength returning to them, ignoring the flesh.

A medley of shouts and barks disturbed the feast. There

was more than one dog this time, and with the voice Boru
had seemed to recognize were others.

"There it is! There's two of 'em! Look at the white
one! Don't fire yet! You'll hit the sheep!"

The dogs were raging beyond the fence, struggling to get
through. As they succeeded and rushed across the corral,
Boru leaped the rails once more. A spurt of flame came
from the opposite side of the inclosure, followed by a report
and the whistle of a bullet that spatted into the timber as
he topped it.

The scene of the night he had fled from the circus, pursued by men and horses, flashed back to Boru in one vivid
second. He remembered the pursuit in the sage of Tamarack Flat, his swim across the river, the jets of fire, the
sound of the guns, and the missiles that he had so narrowly
escaped.

Eighteen feet to the leap, he raced across the frozen snow
to the orchard. A second shot sounded, then another, as
he bounded up the hill, but no more bullets came near him.
The dogs still barked, and there was a confused noise of
shouting as he stood, panting, looking back at the pursuit
and waiting for his mate.

He saw her coming up to him slowly, floundering heavily
through the snow, two dogs in barking pursuit. One of

them stopped at the sound of a shrill whistle, hesitated, and turned back. The other, a mongrel hound, with more bravery than discretion, came on. The she-wolf turned at bay as Boru loped down to join her. Before he reached her there was a scuffle in the snow, a yelp from the hound, and the latter turned and scurried down the hill in terror, dragging one badly bitten leg.

The she-wolf lay on her side in the snow. Boru saw a stain of scarlet slowly spreading on her white fur behind her shoulder, where a bullet had gone home. Her strength was spent, and she could only lie and look at her mate with eyes that were fast losing their sight under the death glaze.

Below, the men were calling in their dogs. The pursuit was over in the belief that the marauders had been driven off and had made good their escape, despite the protestations of the man who had fired.

Boru, troubled at the condition of his mate, who lay very still, with legs and neck far outstretched, her breath coming in gasps that melted little furrows in the snow, licked the wound in her shoulder, then nuzzled her chin, whining as she gave no response. Convulsive shudders shook her body, and she closed her eyes. Boru nipped gently at her ears. Alarm took possession of him, and he dropped his muzzle to hers, which was dry and feverish. Foam had gathered in the corners of her jaws, and blood was oozing through

THE FULL SENSE OF HIS BEREAVEMENT TOOK SUDDEN POS-
SESSION OF BORU. HE STOOD AND GAVE FULL VENT TO HIS
GRIEF IN LONG HOWLS, CARELESS OF SAFETY, OF ANYTHING BUT
THE OVERFLOWING MEASURE OF HIS LOSS

it to the snow. He licked her nose with his warm tongue and whined again. She tried to raise her head and opened her eyes. The light of love shone through their dull amber and flickered as the life went out of them. Her tongue met his caressingly for a second, she gave one sigh, her body shook in one long tremor, then her head dropped heavily in the snow, the tongue protruding a little, her legs became rigid and her breath stopped.

The full sense of his bereavement took sudden possession of Boru. In desperation he licked her unresponsive face and burrowed his muzzle beneath her neck in a vain attempt to arouse her. He licked the wound once more, whimpering the while. The blood had ceased to flow and was already congealing. Already her body was stiffening in the cold air. And so he stood and gave full vent to his grief in long howls, careless of safety, of anything but the overflowing measure of his loss.

In a few minutes a light from a lantern danced over the ground at the foot of the hill and the dogs commenced to bark again. The voices of the men in discussion came clearly to him through the crisp night. The flash of a shot showed by the corral, the report echoed between the hills, and a bullet furrowed a long groove in the snow ten feet away from him. Another followed, passing between Boru and the body of his mate. He loped reluctantly uphill

again to the ridge.   With one more shot, the firing ceased.
The dogs barked a final defiance.

"They won't come back again in a hurry.   If they do,
I'll be ready for them."

The tone of the voice sent a thrill through Boru, penetrating his grief.   It was strangely familiar.   Once it had
been the voice of a friend, he fancied, though in the turmoil
of his sorrow he could not place it.   Now it was that of
an enemy who had robbed him of happiness.

"I hit the white one, I'm sure of it."

It was the other man talking now.   Boru's hair bristled,
and he growled deep in his throat.   Presently he stole
downhill again to his dead mate, sniffed against hope, and
lay down beside her in the snow.   He did not howl again,
fearful that the men might force him to leave her.

The night slowly passed until the Big Dipper had
wheeled its bowl below the farther hill.   The stars shiv-
ered and paled as the sky turned gray, then faintly pink,
in the east.   Boru rose stiffly, warned by the hurrying dawn.
The philosophy of the wild taught him that nothing he
could do would bring his mate back again and that death
was an issue to be faced stoically.   To remain longer was
folly.   The instinct of safety dominated his loneliness,
and, with a heavy heart, he plodded up to the ridge.   He

looked back once. There was only a heap of white fur that made a blur above the snow.

By the time the sun was well above the hills Boru had reached the den in the cliffs above the lake. He entered and lay there through the day, brooding and lonely. In the late afternoon he dozed off, and woke for the moment forgetful of his loss, expectant to find his mate beside him. The den suddenly seemed abhorrent to him in the realization of his desolation, and he trotted out to the ledge of rocks that overlooked the lake where they had watched their whelps at play. He crouched in the sunset, looking across the lake, the idea of revenge slowly dulling the edge of his grief. It was a mixture of motives that inspired his desire for vengeance. There was the strangely familiar tone of the man's voice, the man who had been an active agent in taking his mate from him, there was the memory of her lying, stiff, in the snow, unresponsive to his caresses, and back of these, spurred by his hunger, the recollection of the taste of the hot blood of the sheep he had killed.

He made up his mind for action. As soon as it was dark he would set out for the ridge above the ranch and for the last time see his mate. Then he would wait, for, quickened by the voice of the men, he recalled his old knowledge of human ways—wait until the light in the window went out. Then he would leap the fence once more and kill—kill till he had slaughtered every one of those blatting creatures—a toll of fifty lives for her one. Afterward, he might satisfy his hunger when he had glutted his revenge. If the dogs interfered, so much the better. If the men came!—he had been fired at before and not been hurt—he cared little if he was, if he could reach one of them first.

While he waited his brain cells, responding to his mood, flicked off the film of the months they had spent together, the wooing, the coming of the cubs, his fight to protect them from the eagle, hunting forays and fights, the fire, the battle with the pack, the cloudburst, a long array of joys and perils, victories and disasters shared together, and his resolution strengthened.

The lake grew dark, the ridges blurred against the sky, and still he lay there motionless, his head between his paws. Then the stars pricked out and the water mirrored them. Boru rose, stretched himself, and went off at a steady trot, a moving blot in the gray night, down the mountain toward the valley farm.

The snow was falling before he reached the crest of the ridge above the little orchard and the ranch. Through its veil he could barely distinguish the buildings. But the light showed through the flakes, and he halted, with his gums exposed in a snarl. The dogs were silent as he picked up his trail again and started downhill to where he had left the body of the she-wolf. Suddenly he stopped. The air held a scent that thrilled him with a dread he could not fathom. A few steps farther and the mystery was revealed. The body was gone. In its place was a dark stain that the snow was as yet powerless to cover. Heading down the hill was the indistinct trace where something heavy had been dragged over the snow.

Boru followed it to where it ended in a little gulch almost leveled by the recent snowfall. There he began to dig, slowly at first, then throwing the snow in powdery heaps behind the powerful action of his legs. Soon he exposed a sight that sickened him for the moment, then filled him with a blind rage that checked his involuntary howl of sorrow. It was the flayed carcass of the she-wolf!

The snow drifted down faster as if hastening to shroud the pitiful sight. Boru, intent upon retaliation, instinct and reason alike unhinged by the horror of it all, plunged on with great leaps, breaking through the snow crust with the thrust of his haunches, through the trees of the orchard, down to the corral, ignoring the protection of the creek bed and its bordering willows.

He leaped the bars without faltering in his stride, intent upon running amuck among the sheep. The corral was empty. Baffled, Boru raced round the inclosure. The odor was strong where they had been herded through the entrance despite the fresh layer of snow. The gate was barred, and Boru jumped the obstacle, following the trail to a barn where the rancher had sheltered the sheep for the night, mindful of the possibility of more wolves.

Round the structure the wolfhound ranged, seeking entrance. Baffled, he stopped, looking angrily at the light in the window. He went slowly toward it, uncertain of his next move. Something fluttered on top of the snow between the barns. As Boru neared it, it squawked and tried to escape. He saw it was a bird, larger than a grouse, that seemed wounded, unable to fly or run. His empty stomach shouted for the food, and his mouth watered. With a bound, he reached it, stifling the squawking with the quick snap of his jaws. As his teeth met through the feathers upon the warm flesh something closed on his hind leg like a vise, high up on the hock. He whirled, and pain stabbed him while the thing held him hard with a dead pull that threw him on his side, panting. He could see nothing, the enemy that had attacked him was invisible, hidden beneath the snow. He doubled his supple body and slashed viciously, his teeth clashing against the jaws of a steel trap. He bit at it repeatedly till his jaws were bleeding. Terror possessed him and he thrashed upon the snow in a vain effort at escape. Exhausted at last, he lay still, his

heart thumping wildly, his lungs laboring for air, the dead
hen that had baited the trap flung to one side.   The agony
of the metal fangs sinking relentlessly into flesh and sinew
roused him to renewed attempts, but the links of the chain
that fastened the trap to a heavy log held, and the steel
jaws were immovable.

His legs grew numb at last.   Half starved as he was,
his strength ebbed quickly, and the cold of the night penetrated his body.   Soon he lay still, hopelessly awaiting
the end, his limbs growing as stiff as those of his mate lying on the hillside, the snow wreathing a common pall for
both of them.   All pain had gone, and a delicious languor
stole over him.

The door of the ranch house opened and closed, and the
lantern light swung in the hand of a man who went to the
fence of the garden patch and took from it a white skin
hanging limp over the palings.

"I'd better be taking this in," the man said.   " 'Tis a
fine rug it'll make.   It's a shame to lose the head, but
there's twenty-dollars bounty the boss'll be wantin', an' that
means turnin' in the ears an' muzzle.   'Twas a lucky shot
for him, but if the trap gets the other one I'll be even with
him.   I'll take a look at it before I turn in."

He put back the wolfskin on the fence and walked toward the spot between the barns where he had baited the

trap with the live chicken in the hope of catching the big wolf that had escaped the night before.

Some last remnant of consciousness lingering in Boru rallied the brain with a warning call to action. He raised his head feebly, shaking off the snow, and snarled at the oncoming lantern. With an effort, he roused himself, twisting his body to present a front to the enemy, his haunches flattened, the lower leg bound by the tenacious trap.

The man drew a pistol from his hip pocket and cocked it.

"He's a big divvle," he said. "Nigh dead with the cold. He'd be dead by mornin', but I'll put him out of his misery."

He lifted the lantern in his left hand and took aim. The falling snow bothered his sight, and he stepped closer to the snarling animal. Boru faced him without a sound, lifting his head and regarding him with steady eyes, waiting for him to get near enough for one desperate slash.

The man stopped and held the lantern closer to the captive's head.

"By all the Saints!" he cried. " 'Tis no wolf at all. It's a dog. By the powers, it's Boru!"

He uncocked the pistol and replaced it in his pocket.

"Whist, Boru!" he said. "Don't ye know me? Ye

poor divvle! Killin' sheep, are ye? That's murder, my son. 'Tis not that ye were meant for."

Boru recognized him. At last the voice held full meaning. It was Dempsey, the drunken Irish ex-trainer who had shown him the wolf in the circus menagerie.

Dempsey, discharged at the end of the season and now a ranch hand, looked at him whimsically.

"An' I thought ye were the same as twenty dollars in my pocket," he said. "Those ears of yours would never pass for a wolf's, my boy. Ye poor divvle! It's hungry ye were when ye killed the sheep, I'm thinkin'. An' ye're Irish, like meself. I'll not be killin' ye."

He looked back toward the ranch. The light in the window had vanished.

"Will ye lave the sheep alone, if I let ye loose?" he asked, as he bent over the wolfhound. "Aisy, now," he added, as Boru growled. "I'm not goin' to hurt ye—I'm helping ye."

Boru sensed the kindliness of the tone. His rancor had died out of him with the hours of freezing cold. He remembered Dempsey as a friend, and as the Irishman warily stooped to pat his shoulder, he mutely accepted the caress.

Dempsey brushed the snow from the dog's chilled body and found the trap tightly clenched upon the torn leg.

"Lie still for a minute, Boru," he said, and set his strength to open the jawed hinges. Freed, Boru lay quiet while Dempsey gently and deftly chafed his wounded leg, then rubbed his body briskly with snow.

"Up with ye, lad!" he said encouragingly.

Boru stood staggeringly on his stiffened legs and gratefully licked the Irishman's hand. Anger had gone out of him. Once more he recognized man as a protector, not an enemy.

"I can't take ye in," said Dempsey. "The boss'll not forgive ye the sheep. But he can afford to forget them, an' ye're worth the flock. So ye must shift for yourself the best ye can. Ye're welcome to the chicken."

He picked up the trap and tossed it to one side, taking up the lantern.

"Good-by, Boru," he said. "And good luck to ye."

As he reached the fence he looked back. He could dimly see the wolf-hound against the snow, gazing after him.

"When he gets the chicken into him he'll cheer up," he said. "I hope he has sense enough to make tracks before mornin'."

CHAPTER FOUR

FRIENDSHIP AND HATE

HIGH up on the snow-covered flanks of the mountain a black dot was slowly moving downward, the only animate object in view. No wind disturbed the frozen particles of the snow crust over which the black dot progressed so tardily. The breathless air was ominous, and held the bite of a Montana midwinter. The sun was tarnished by a wrack of gray cloud that sped southward in ragged battalions driven by the gale that swept the higher levels. From the crests of the Snow Mountains that begin in Park County, Montana, and drive their southerly spurs into Buffalo Plateau, in the northwestern corner of the Yellowstone National Park, Wyoming, snow banners waved their danger signals from the topmost peaks.

No snow was falling, and the ridges stood out sharply severe against the slaty sky. The moving speck crept on, stopping sometimes, then crawling on again toward timber line in painful but constant progress. It was Boru, dragging one hind leg that furrowed the snow in his trail, numb with the bitterness of the unsheltered morning, weak from starvation, gamely struggling until the last spark of vitality should falter and die.

He had had a hard fight of it for a week, traveling south as best he could because that way was the easiest with its gradual trend to lower levels. The climbs he had been forced to make occasionally had brought agony to his leg. A deep wound, still raw, ringed it above the hock where the jaws of the trap that had caught him in his unsuccessful raid upon the sheep of the rancher who had killed his mate, the white wolf, had bitten hard and deep; and he had been badly handicapped since Dempsey, ex-trainer of lions, friend of the days when Boru was part and parcel of a wandering circus, had forced the trap apart and given him another chance for life and liberty. He had devoured the chicken that had baited the fateful trap, and the scant meal had given him heart to limp up the mountain from the valley ranch. He made fair progress at first, until the swelling of his stiffened limb made him lie up for two days, licking at the wound between sleeps, sheltered from the weather in a cave on the leeward side of the pass that led southward through the saddle of the Snow Mountains.

Desperate hunger sent him out at last to find that fortune still held some favors for him. A flock of snow geese were flying in a V above him, making the pass, driving for Yellowstone Lake and immunity, urged by human destructiveness—though this Boru could not know—to a haven provided by man.

The leader, with the alarm of the shots and hail of pellets that had greeted the flock in a valley lake two hours before still dominating his small brain and speeding his flight to more than a mile a minute, stretched his long neck still farther as he caught sight of the plateau far below, darkly cleft by the cañon of the Yellowstone River, and saw the gleaming harborage of the lake. He swung sharply, with a *honk-honk* of guidance to his followers, and swept on sturdy pinions due south.

Boru watched the trailing band with vague envy at their speed and keener disappointment at their safety from his hungry jaws. At more honking, he lifted his ears. Flying low and clumsily, a straggler of the flock, trumpeting plaintively to its swifter fellows, came beating through the gap. As Boru caught sight of the brant, its strength failed, and, with a choking squawk, it slanted helplessly down, the still-spread wings plowing into the snow, where it lay prone with stretched neck limp, the life dulled in the black, beady eyes, the crimson stain on its breast, where the rancher's buckshot had torn its way, splotching the snow beneath it.

The big gray wolfhound floundered on three legs to the providential victim. In a few seconds nothing was left of the brant but scattered feathers and a beak. Boru, revived and heartened, crossed the ridge and began the long trail downward, following slowly, painfully, step after step, the direction taken by the swiftly flying snow geese, already out of sight.

Then the real siege started. Ridge after ridge still stretched before him, snow-covered, with the gaunt bones of the mountains protruding here and there. The fuel of his meal slowly died down, and the pads of his feet cracked and grew raw with the steady travel over the crust. At night, he curled up in the lee of barren rocks and dozed till at daybreak he again forced his stiffened limbs to drag him on.

The third day after he had crossed the pass he saw the blue-black line of the timber below, and far ahead of him, and in the knowledge of shelter and the hope of food made shift to mend his speed. The frozen surface that hurt his feet was his salvation. Soft snow would have sapped the last remnant of his strength. Snowfall would soon have buried him in a drift.

Down toward the trees he stumbled, often resting panting heavily in the scant air of the high altitude, dragging himself sometimes on his belly, but always nearing the timber line.

The sky grew blacker, snuffing out the sun at last. Boru's creeping shadow vanished. It appeared impossible for him to fill his lungs. The air seemed to have vanished, leaving a vacuum in which he gasped for breath. All the strength seemed to have gone from his limbs, but still he crept on, foot after foot, then inch by inch, until at last he reached the verge of the trees, crawled on a little, and lay panting, gathering the remnants of his strength and will for further exertion.

It was good to be beneath the friendly pines, after the days of unbroken snow. They seemed to greet him and promise him food and shelter. There was snow on the ground, but it was not deep, and the boughs were green above him where the top branches thatched the rest. Better than all, there were trails on the snow, triangular imprints of grouse and ptarmigan, the slurred tracks of rabbits and crisper marks of creatures whose pads were tipped with claws.

He was lame, and staggering from weakness, dizzy and dim-sighted, but where there was food in the larder there was always hope of securing it, and Boru kept on.

Suddenly he stopped, ears lifting, muzzle up, and nostrils open, his sight keen once more, flattening his gray form against the bole of a pine, indistinguishable, motionless. There was a clearing in the forest where a fire had killed the older trees, and the second growth had permitted the underbrush to flourish. It was all bare twigs and branches now, snow-weighted, with here and there a stubborn dead leaf still clinging. But Boru had sensed movement among the brush, coming his way, and he waited. The branches shook, tossing the snow from them as they were forced aside, and a rabbit broke cover at full speed, its long ears flattened down, making frantic leaps over the frozen surface.

Its path was at a tangent from Boru's tree, and he knew himself too lame to cut off its retreat, but a swifter enemy pursued it, gliding along in relentless chase, a weasel, white as the snow in its winter coat, darting anglewise on its prey. The rabbit gave a shrill cry of terror as the weasel sprang at its throat, fastening blood-thirsty jaws in a death grip.

The tragedy ended only a dozen feet from Boru's hiding place. Unmindful of his wounded leg, he cleared the space at a bound. The startled weasel whirled angrily, ready to fight; then, stricken with sudden dismay at the great form straddling him, the red mouth bristling with white teeth that slashed downward, whisked indignantly away as Boru's watering jaws claimed the rabbit.

It was only a mouthful, as Boru bolted it, fur and flesh complete, but it was like an extra ammunition belt to a beleaguered garrison, and it renewed the wolfhound's lease on life.

PERPLEXED, HE HALTED, HATING TO RUN, UNCERTAIN HOW
TO FACE THE DANGER AND AVERT IT IN HIS FAVOUR. THE NEXT
MOMENT HE WAS THE HUB OF A CIRCLE OF PONDEROUS,
LOWERING HEADS

Late that afternoon, he came to the edge of the woods on the verge of low cliffs that fell to a plateau shut in by mountains. The sun was low, and he prospected for a place to sleep and rest, too tired for further travel. The trunk of a fallen tree promised shelter. He scratched away the snow from its lower side, to prepare a bed, and stopped, snuffing at what his paws had uncovered, a pile of grasshoppers wedged under the hollow of the log where they had sought refuge from the frost. There were thousands in the heap, dead, shriveled, but, to Boru's famine-sharpened palate, a feast. He crunched the crisp morsels until he had devoured the last wing cover. Then, with his belly filled and warmed, if not overnourished, circled thrice, and curled himself up to sleep.

Boru awoke ravenous. His substantial supper had long been assimilated by his craving system, and, while it had served to revive his vitality, it had also whetted his appetite to the point where, lame and still weak as he was, he would have fought a whole family of bears for a fish head.

The sight that greeted him as he reached the brow of the plateau cliffs excited his hunting instinct and craft beyond control. Browsing on the herbage beneath the snow were a score of creatures with dark shaggy coats and enormous mane-hung shoulders that seemed to weight their heads to the ground. They were a part of the Yellowstone herd of bison, grazing contentedly, as if aware of the protection extended them by the law.

To Boru they represented so much meat, warm and red with blood, ready for the killing. Two of them were calves, one of which was lying down not a quarter of a mile from the cliffs.

This Boru selected for his breakfast. He had no idea of their speed, but he knew his own present limitations, and prepared to stalk the yearling. He had no thought of resistance. He had never met anything yet on hoofs that would face him except a buck at bay, and these creatures he placed as some kin to deer. They had hoofs, not claws, that was certain, and their short horns did not appear particularly formidable. He found a gully that, with a leap here and there, was negotiable for a descent to the plateau, and made his way down, anticipating an easily gained and eminently satisfactory breakfast.

In the excitement of the hunt, Boru's leg stopped bothering him. The lust of the sport as well as the imminent prospect of a full meal sent the blood coursing swiftly through the injured muscles and stimulated them to perfect response. Belly to the ground, he crept closer to the buffalo calf, gliding from sage clump to sage clump silent and unseen by the unsuspecting yearling. The last bush that would cover him was within twenty yards of the victim. Boru knew he could cover that in four or five leaps, and he fixed his eyes on the point of his attack. He decided to hamstring the calf. It looked bulkier than he had thought it at a distance, and the creature appeared to have no neck, the head so sunk between the shoulders that he was not sure of a successful spring at the throat.

With his mouth slavering with desire, he made ready for his leaping rush into the open. That would startle the calf to its feet, and give him the opening to slash the hocks, and then worry the life out of its throat while the rest of the herd stampeded in terror.

But in the zest of the chase and the urge of hunger, Boru had forgotten one thing—the wind. And he knew nothing of the keen scent of the bison. A puff of wind gave them warning even as he charged. In a moment they had turned their massive heads toward him, their little eyes shining wickedly in the matted fronts. Even the calf had whirled swiftly, and stood with head lowered to meet the intruder.

Boru kept going, expecting to see them break in terror. To his amazement, the creatures stood their ground, snorting and pawing the ground. Then, with a roaring bellow, they came thundering toward him, converging on him from a dozen angles, suddenly formidable, enraged at the presumption of what they thought a gray wolf, a little larger than the ordinary, an enemy, indeed, but one readily defeated.

The tables were turned. In place of a frightened rabble and a helpless victim, a dozen monsters, assuming gigantic proportions, were bearing down upon him, menacing him with being crushed to a pulp beneath their trampling hoofs. Even the calf seemed unafraid. Perplexed, he halted, hating to run, uncertain how to face the danger and avert it in his favor. The next moment he was the hub of a circle of ponderous lowering heads. Something thudded into his ribs, lifted him, tossed him high in air, to come down, sprawling, on the snow twenty feet away. As he scrambled to his feet, he saw the monsters charging him at incredible speed, and fled for the cliffs, leaping the sage clumps, impelled by the snorts and bellows of the brutes as they plunged after him in swift pursuit. He reached the gully barely ahead, and raced up it, springing and clawing his way up the rocks that blocked his progress, and proved an effectual barricade to the infuriated bison. Boru did not stop his ignominious flight until he reached the summit of the cliffs, bruised and breathless, and saw his conquerors below, pawing impotently in their rage, and bellowing their desire to reach him.

Boru was in evil plight. His whole side throbbed and

stiffened where the battering-ram of the bison's head had hurled him aloft. In the dejection of defeat, the pain and numbness in his leg reasserted itself. The demands upon his last reserves of strength left him faint and weak. Assured that his assailants could not mount the cliff, he made his way to his bed by the log, and dropped exhausted, sinking into a torpor that was half sleep and half unconsciousness. And, while he lay, his spirit once more marshaled the crimson corpuscles of his blood and undauntedly prepared for still another effort to preserve life.

It was high noon when he recovered sensibility. The blood in his veins ran scalding hot, his mouth seemed full of dust, and he longed for water to assuage the thirst that racked him. It was a week since he had tasted real water. The snow that he had licked from time to time was only a mockery now. He wanted water, a running stream of it, where he could plunge his burning muzzle and drink and drink again until his thirst was appeased. His hunger was lost in the fire of the fever that possessed him.

He rose dizzily on limbs that held no feeling, and walked with short unsteady steps to the edge of the cliff. The bison were grazing out on the plateau a mile or more away. Boru had no heart for further adventure in that direction, but to the right, and westward, he marked a line of willows and alders that bordered a black line winding across the snow. It meant water. To cross the open plateau was certain death from the bison, and he made his way, tottering, along the cliffs at the edge of the trees. Their formation was that of a horseshoe, the curve toward the plain. As Boru followed the arc, he was hidden after a while from the bison, and this time his experience-sharpened faculties bade him give notice to the wind, which was in his favor.

Selecting a spot where the cliff sloped less sharply, he started downward toward the water, still a long way off across the plain that tilted gradually toward the stream. At every step progress grew more difficult; occasionally both hind legs failed him, and dragged. His side was numb, and the paralysis slowly gained mastery. The snow seemed to rise and fall in waves before him, and often his legs collapsed, and he flopped helplessly down, only to struggle on again, whipped by the burning torment of his thirst, sustained by the will for life that dominates the creatures of the wild, until the broken body can no longer contain the resolute spirit.

As he grew weaker the dizziness passed and he saw the willows very far away and knew he could not reach them. He willed his limbs to carry him, but the message failed to leave the brain, the last citadel of his vitality. He pitched forward and lay, his out-stretched head pointing to the water he could see, but could not reach. He was even too feeble now to lick snow, content to lie with eyes bright from fever, too tired for thinking, too exhausted for subconscious memories, impotent, but free from cowardice, patiently waiting for the end.

On the western side of Hellroaring Creek where the up-slope was thickly set with timber, two men stood close to the fringe of the trees. They wore snowshoes. Each carried a rifle, a thing forbidden in the park unless sealed by the cavalry patrol. But the mechanisms of these 30-30's were ready for action, and the men carried clips of ammunition in the belts beneath their deerskin coats. All the metal parts were dulled, and at either muzzle was affixed a Maxim silencer.

Their ear-tabbed caps were of fur; their long skirted coats met leggings of deerskin tanned with the hair on. At a little distance, when crouching or on all fours, it would be hard to distinguish them from deer, even with a field glass. The costume was a dangerous one for hunters, but in the park where bullets were tabooed, there was little risk. The skins served a double purpose in their case, not merely as a means for approaching game, but for self-protection. The men were poachers on the national preserve, taking advantage of the abundance of game that sought the security of the park, guarded by four troops of cavalry in the summer, two in the winter.

The elder of the two, black-bearded, shorter, and more heavily built than his blond companion, had a leather case slung across his shoulders.   Through the glasses that fitted it, he gazed intently across the stream.

"It's a gray wolf," he said, after a lengthy survey.   "Biggest I've seen.   Looks badly crippled.   I've a mind to take a shot at it.   His pelt ought to be a whopper.   I'll try it from here."

"Aw, what's the use?" demurred the other.   "You'll have to cross the open to get it."

"There's no one patrolling this end of the park to-day," replied the short man, sweeping the plateau and its bordering hills with the glasses.

"How d'ye know?   They ain't no use in fool risks. We're five miles over the park line."

The other looked at him scornfully.

"Don't ye know what day it is?" he said.   "It's Christmas, you fool.   They're all hugging the fire at the fort. Trust 'em."

The younger man passed over the slurring tone.

"Christmas!" he said.   "Christmas Day!"   His gray eyes looked wistfully across the snow.   "A hell of a Christmas for us!   And the folks home eatin' turkey an' mince pies an' the kiddies playin' with their toys.   My God, Simmonds, it———"

His voice trembled, and he stopped, swallowing the lump that rose in his throat.

"Ah, shut up! You make me sick!" The bearded man spoke in a harsh guttural. "If it's presents you want," he went on, "there's one over on the snow. Twenty dollars bounty for his scalp at Bozeman. Ye can get all the turkey an' mince pies ye want with that an' something to wash it down with. The whisky's gettin' low."

Jim Edler laughed not over-enthusiastically. He held no great affection for Simmonds, who had limped into his camp early in the fall with a sprained ankle. After Edler had doctored him as best he could, the two had joined forces, living after snowfall in a shack that Edler had pre-empted and repaired. The enforced constancy of their companionship had begun to wear upon their tempers, though Simmonds flared up the more readily and the of-tener.

Boru saw the two figures as they came forward from the trees. They walked upright on two legs, and he knew them for men. Once he had fled from man's dominion, reveling in his freedom, believing every man's hand against him. Now, in his extremity, the old belief in man's protection engendered through many generations came back. Demp-sey, too, had been kind, he remembered.

He raised his head with difficulty as Simmonds lifted his

rifle and sighted.   Boru barked, at first with feeble hoarse-
ness, then with deep resonance that shook his tired chest.
Back came an answering bark.   Boru's ears lifted and he
barked again, not knowing the dog he imagined with the
men was only the ghost raised by the echo of his own voice.

Edler touched Simmonds on the arm.

"Don't shoot," he said.   "It's a dog."

"A dog!   You're crazy.   What d'ye figure it—eight
hundred yards?"

Edler struck up the rifle.

"Sure it's a dog," he protested.   "Listen to that.
Wolves don't bark."

It was Edler who came to Boru's rescue, Simmonds de-
claring a crippled dog was not worth powder and shot.

"We can't use him," he said, after Edler prevailed upon
him to cross the creek.   "He'll only give us away.   Finish
him up if you want to.   He's no good, anyhow.   He can't
walk."

"He got here, didn't he?" asked Edler.   "He's just all
in, that's all.   Got a nasty place on his leg here, and it
looks as if he had a rib or two stove in, but he's worth a
dozen dead dogs, ain't you, old chap?"

Boru's dark-brown eyes to which the luster of hope was
returning, met the kindly gray ones of Edler, and he made
shift to feebly stir his tail.

"'Atta boy," said Edler. "You've sure been in some mix-up, dog, and it's a long day since you had a square meal, or I am badly mistaken."

Boru watched him lying contentedly as a deft hand passed lightly over his body, touching his injuries gently, and ending the inspection by scratching him behind the ears. A sense of fealty glowed within him, and he licked Edler's hand with his parched tongue. Meanwhile Simmonds had hunkered down on the snow, searching the distance with his glasses.

"Well?" he asked at last. "What you aimin' to do with yore Christmas present? Tote it home on yore back?"

"I'm goin' to give him a drink first of all," said Elder. "A real one."

He took off his fur cap and converted it into a primitive bowl, half filling it at the creek with the water Boru craved. Into this he poured the contents of his canteen, while Simmonds growled disapproval.

"There ain't none too much hooch left to be wastin' any of it on a dog," he said. "Not at the price we have to pay fer it."

"My money bought it," returned Edler shortly.

Boru sniffed at the mixture, but lapped up the liquid eagerly, while Edler held the cap. The potion coursed through his veins with a strange, delicious sense of exhilaration and returning power. He started to get to his feet, but Edler softly, but firmly, kept him in his position by the pressure of a hand on his neck.

"Hold on, partner," he said. "Wait till you get something solid in you. You ain't no objection to my givin' him my lunch, have ye?" he asked, satirically turning to Simmonds, who shrugged his shoulders.

Stimulated by the whisky and water, Boru devoured the elk meat and sour-dough bread that Edler gave him, then blissfully resigned himself to the gentle massage bestowed upon him, lying on his side with half closed eyes. After all his travail it was good to render himself up to protection, and in his heart he vowed a debt of gratitude.

"Now then, old chap," said Edler. "See how your pins'll hold you up."

Boru stood up, his vigor swiftly mounting with his stayed stomach and the kick of the spirits that had restored the circulation of his blood. Legs well apart, he shook himself free of the snow and pushed his head into Edler's hand, leaning his weight against him to express his thanks.

It was a long trail for Boru to the cabin across the park line but he followed Edler gratefully, in the conviction that his troubles were over. After all he had gone through, especially the loss of his mate, freedom seemed a petty thing to give up for protection, and, greatest of all, companionship.   So he staggered along, cheered by Edler's encouraging words, forced to rest at more and more frequent intervals, fighting off increasing drowsiness until at last they reached the two-roomed shack of sodded logs, and, with a grunt, he dropped to the floor beside the open fire where logs were glowing, and achieved temporary oblivion.

For two weeks he stayed close to the cabin, well fed with meat that soon made a new dog of him.   Despite Edler's fears, the buffalo's toss had not broken his ribs, and the poacher daily treated his injured leg with bear grease and a massage that rapidly restored it to full strength.   In return Boru registered gratitude in his brain ready to be redeemed at the first opportunity.

It did not take him long to recognize the growing enmity between the two men.   Close quarters and opposing natures frazzled the edge of their tempers.   Days passed without their interchanging more than a few words, and when the weather kept them within the cabin, its inclemency seemed to communicate itself to the interior despite the log fire and the stove in the inner room where they slept in built-up bunks.

Edler made a chum and confidant of Boru, and Simmonds, to show his opposition to his partner in a dozen petty ways, showed his dislike of the dog, to whom he transferred a goodly share of his growing hatred for Edler.   He was,

in his heart, afraid of the great wolfhound, nor did he desire open rupture with Edler, but he would spill Boru's
water as if by accident or kick his half-gnawed bone into
the ashes while Boru watched him with slow anger crim-
soning his eyes, repressing the growl in his throat, avoiding
trouble for Edler's sake.

Also, Simmonds possessed a supernatural power that
gripped the very soul of Boru in a misery that left him
helplessly protesting, bound in a spell that he could not
muster courage to break. Simmonds discovered his mastery by accident; but, once assured of it, reveled in the
torture.

He had brought a violin with him from wherever he had
come, and, in the evenings and on weather-bound days, he
would play it by the hour. It had been company for both
the men at first, and even now Edler, equally with Simmonds, enjoyed the old melodies that brought up happier,
younger days, despite the homesickness they invoked. Simmonds played well in an uncultivated way, and at times
he improvised strange airs that fitted the wild weather
without and the wild spirits within.

Boru liked the music at first. Far more keenly sensitive to vibration than either of the men, it at once thrilled
and soothed him. Then, one night, in his improvisations,
Simmonds fingered high harmonics. The shrill notes

stabbed Boru's sensibility like daggers that bored and twisted in the wounds they made. He howled in involuntary anguish. Edler tried to soothe him, and Simmonds cursed, then laughed and repeated the phrase. Boru howled again, raised on his forelegs, his throat stretched to the full, quivering with emotion.

"They's no sense in tormentin' the dog," said Edler angrily.

"Tormentin'? Who's tormentin' him?" retorted Simmonds. "He's a musical hound. Listen to him. He's plumb in key."

"Well, I'm not stuck on that squeaking myself," said Edler. "Sounds like a screech owl in distress."

Simmonds stopped his harmonics for the time, but after that he took delight in arousing Boru after playing softer melodies by suddenly repeating them in the higher octaves. He seldom did this when Edler was present, and then pretended he had forgotten; but, when he was alone in the cabin with the dog, he delighted in the refined torture.

Boru sensed the deliberate malice. He tried to control his feelings but, the moment the piercing notes started, he had to give vent to the howls that came involuntarily from his protesting spirit. Then Simmonds would change the air, and Boru would lie, glowering, till the soft tones soothed him, and Simmonds would laugh and put away his violin.

One day the two men quarreled over it, and Edler warned Simmonds that he was playing with fire.

"Some day the dog'll get you by the throat," he said. "And it'll serve you right if he chokes the life out of you."

One hot word led to another, and soon Edler swung out of the cabin to attend to some traps he had set. Simmonds watched him through the window. Then he took up the fiddle.

"Now you an' me'll have a little session," he said to Boru, who watched him handling the instrument and growled softly.

"I can play on you just like I play on this fiddle," said Simmonds. "You're growling, are you? I'll soon stop that."

He set the violin to his chin and started to play in minor melodies that were indescribably hypnotic to Boru's sensitive nerves. Simmonds bowed softly, first the air, and then in double-chorded harmony. At the close of "My Old Kentucky Home," Boru lay with his head on his forepaws, eyes half closed in ecstasy at the croon of the old tune.

"Now then," said Simmonds, "look out!"

There were phrases that particularly affected Boru, and these the man commenced to play.

Boru set himself to withstand their influence, his eyes fixed on the mocking light in the man's. As surely as saliva would flow, unbidden, in his jaws at certain suggestions of appetite, so the high notes set his spirit shivering. His diaphragm quivered, the bow seemed playing on his very heart-strings, and subconsciously, against his will, at the command of something that held possession of him, he threw up his muzzle and howled.

Simmonds kept on, sawing persistently on certain notes, laughing till the tears ran down his face, while Boru, on his haunches, red-eyed, the soul within him torn asunder, sent out howl after howl in weird concert.

Simmonds began to play discords.   Boru's mood changed to fury.   His brain, in indignant revolt, urged him to spring at the jeering man, but still the music compelled him, broke the coördination of his nerve centers, and stopped the summons of his mind to assert himself.   Trembling with rage, the moisture from his mouth spotting the floor, he had perforce to howl his heart out.

Simmonds sawed on the E string, his finger high on the frets.   First a high G, then a shrieking, purposely discordant tone slurred between it and the A above.

Suddenly the worn string snapped, and with it the tension of Boru's control. His howl changed to a roar of concentrated hatred as, released from the spell, he launched himself straight at Simmonds' throat.

The fiddle clattered to the floor.   Simmonds struck

blindly with his bow, aghast at the swift attack. Boru's bulk, urged by the rage that rose in a flood tide of revenge, struck him full on the chest, and he went down with a crash, trying to keep the ravening jaws from his throat.

The door swung open, and Edler rushed in, calling to the dog. Boru, unheeding, his forepaws planted on his enemy's chest, worried his muzzle through the defending arms, intent upon tearing open the bearded throat. Edler threw his arms about his neck, shouting to him as he tried to drag back the hundred and thirty pounds of angry doghood.

Boru dimly heard him, but fought on. He recognized his friend's voice and forebore to turn and slash at the interferer, but the frenzy to kill his enemy still dominated him.

By main force, Edler lifted the struggling dog in his arms.

"Git up, you fool!" he said to Simmonds, who lay on the floor, his face livid, his eyes staring, the sleeves of his thick coat slashed. "Quick, an' git out of this. I can't hold him much longer."

Simmonds scrambled to all fours and sprang, in crouching leaps, to the door of the inner room, slamming it behind him as he darted through just in time to close it on Boru, who broke from Edler's hold and hurled himself against the barrier.

The door held. Edler talked to the frantic dog soothingly, and presently the quiet, friendly tones had their effect, and Boru's rage slowly subsided.

Edler sat on the rough table, Boru's head on his knee, his tail proclaiming the flag of truce and good-fellowship. For Edler's sake he was willing to forgive if not entirely to forget.

"He's a mongrel, an' you're a thoroughbred, my boy," said Edler, scratching his ears. "He won't do it again, that's certain. He fell plumb on the fiddle an' smashed it to matches. Also, I aim to have a little talk with him.

"You can come out now," he called.

The door opened, and Simmonds' face appeared, white and twitching.

"The dog won't hurt ye," said Edler. "Will ye?"

Simmonds came slowly into the room. Suddenly he snatched his rifle from the wall.

"What are you aimin' to do?" asked Edler, sliding off the table.

"To do——? Kill that damned cur of yours."

Boru had got up and steadfastly watched Simmonds' movements. Deep in his throat he sounded warning, his hair lifting, his gums curling back, and his powerful loins set for another spring.

"Put that up!"

Edler's revolver was in his hand, covering Simmonds, who stood irresolute.

"I'll plug you first if you try it," said Edler. "You brought it on yourself. I heard you as I came up. It was lucky for you I came when I did. You owe me your life. I'll trade it for the dog's. And after this," he went on, "the dog travels with me. I ain't goin' to turn you out, but this is my shack. Me an' the dog'll sleep in the other room after this; you'll bunk out here. Put up the gun!"

"He smashed my fiddle," said Simmonds vindictively.

"You busted it yourself," said Edler. "An' what I said goes. If you don't like it, you can move out. I prefer the dog's comp'ny anyways."

Simmonds' eyes narrowed, and he snarled in his beard. But there was no other shelter handy, and this was midwinter. He forced a laugh and put back the rifle.

"It was my fault," he said. "The dog's all right. Come here, Buck!"

Boru, whose eyes had never wavered in their scrutiny, read the dissembled hate behind the proffered friendship. He turned his back and stalked over to the fireplace, deliberately ignoring the outstretched hand.

The new year came and days melted into weeks, with storms of snow and wind that beset the little cabin and kept its three inmates close-quartered. The cold was intense at that altitude, nearly seven thousand feet above sea level, but there was plenty of wood for the fire and supplies for their simple larder. In good weather the two men cleared the cabin from the drifts that sought to overwhelm it and made short trips on their snowshoes for needed exercise. Sometimes Boru went with Edler when the crust was hard enough to bear him. When the snow was too soft to travel, he would take up his post outside to wait for Edler's return. He never stayed in the cabin alone with Simmonds.

The latter had made several attempts to get on good terms with Boru, but the wolfhound knew the real enmity behind the friendly mask and kept aloof. And the breach between the two men steadily widened. It was tacitly understood that with the coming of spring they would separate. Meanwhile each nursed a growing hatred.

There came a spell in the middle of February when it looked as if the winter had suddenly made up its mind to resign in favor of early spring. On the third day Boru and Edler made a long trip over the hard snow and returned to the cabin to find Simmonds absent. Edler noticed that some of the pelts were missing, but not the bedding or several other articles of Simmonds' belongings.

"I half hoped he'd gone for good," he said to Boru, and the latter wagged his tail in comprehension and agreement.

The next afternoon Simmonds returned without the pelts, but bearing a demijohn of ranch-made liquor for which he had snowshoed fifteen miles each way. That the raw stuff had been freely sampled was evident.

Edler made no comment, and Simmonds helped get supper in the usual silence. He did not offer to share any of the corn liquor which he drank steadily through the evening. When Edler turned in for the night, Simmonds was sitting in front of the fireplace, glowering sullenly into the logs, a tin cup charged with the crude hooch in his hand.

In the middle of the night Boru woke to find the room full of smoke. From the other room came a crackling sound. What air he could draw to his lungs choked him with its pungent heat. He sprang to his feet in alarm, with his brain surging with vivid memories that recalled the forest fire with all its searing flame and smothering smoke through which he and his mate had battled, losing their cubs in the fight. Terror threatened him for the moment. Then, as his faculties asserted themselves with the shaking off of sleep, he reared up to the bunk where Edler lay, half unconscious already from the fumes, and barked loudly at the persistent sleeper.

The smoke thickened, and the crackling grew louder. Boru stripped the blankets from Edler's body with his teeth and seized him by the collar of his shirt, tugging and shaking till he had dragged him partly over the edge of the bunk.

Edler, aroused at last, reeled from the bed half dressed, as he had turned in for the night. He flung open the door and the darkness of the inner room was broken by the light of flames leaping up the fireplace wall. The outer room reeked with the smell of scorching furs and blankets. Across it, head down, Edler staggered to the outer door, fumbling at the bar that fastened it, and, blind and choking, crossed the theshold and fell unconscious in the snow.

Boru went with him, his head still clear from the purer air nearer the floor, and stood over him, licking his face. Then he remembered Simmnods. Ages-old instinct fought with prejudice for a moment and prevailed. He forgot his grudges and remembered only that there was the life of a man to be rescued.

The draft from the open door had fanned the fire, and for a moment he hesitated at the snapping mounting flames. Then he leaped into the burning room. Simmonds lay on the floor, face down, his head cuddled in his arms, overcome more by drink than smoke. Boru wasted no time in barking, but grasped the nearer arm in his powerful jaws and tugged with all his strength at the heavy, inert body.

He moved it jerkily, a few inches at a time, until one of Simmonds' legs caught between the table and a stump that served for chair and held him fast despite Boru's utmost efforts.

He barked and ran to the door to meet Edler, revived by his contact with the snow.   Boru returned to tug at the arm again as Edler set his hands under Simmonds' armpits and so dragged him out of the cabin.

Leaving him in a drift, he gathered great armsful of the compact snow and hurled them, hissing, against the burning logs of the wall and the inner partition.   It was an effective extinguisher, the more as the logs, high-packed with snow on the exterior, were slow to burn.   The damage was not irreparable.   They still had a shelter.

Edler surveyed the ruin in the star-light, with Boru beside him, panting from excitement.   He had not been able to help in putting out the fire save by barking encouragement, but now he muzzled close to Edler and wagged his tail in congratulations.

" 'Tain't often you put out a fire by snowballin' it, eh, Buck?" said Edler, patting him.   "B-r-r-h, it's cold!   I'll get chilblains padding round here in my socks.   Tuck in your tongue and stop laughing at me.   I'm goin' to get my

boots on.   Then we'll tote him inside.   I s'pose he tipped
the jimmyjohn in the fire."

He nodded at Simmonds sprawling in the drift where
Elder had flung him and went into the cabin.

Boru looked at his enemy, breathing heavily, his beard
singed.   It hurt him to see a man, the superior being who
walked erect and could do so many things that he could only
wonder at, helpless in the snow.   Personal injustice set
aside, he walked over to the drunkard and licked his face
with his warm tongue.

There are more than three thousand square miles in
Yellowstone Park, and to thoroughly patrol that territory
with two skeleton troops of cavalry is not a duty easily accomplished.   The park averages over six thousand feet in
altitude, and its wild country is the drifting ground of
snow and ice from October until the end of April.

Up at the northern end of Buffalo Plateau, Simmonds
and Edler ran small risk of molestation.   The majority of
the poachers worked in from the Jackson Hole district,
far to the south, below Yellowstone Lake.

Bears were plentiful in the Yellowstone Lake Preserve,
black and brown, grizzly and cinnamon, but they were all
holed up for the winter, and the two paid their attention
to smaller game, accumulating a fair pile of fox and skunk

and marten and rabbit, with wild cat and mountain lion.
These were good at Deevers, the nearest railway station, for
general supplies and perhaps a little cash. The Yellowstone National Park, tucked away in the northwest corner
of Wyoming, extends a short distance into Montana. Edler's cabin was a scant half mile beyond the park line, and
they preferred to confine their depredations to a limit not
too far from their home base.

They knew exactly where that line ran. On one side
of it they were trespassers, on the other safe in neutral
territory beyond the jurisdiction of the park control.

With Boru's advent their prospects brightened as they
discovered and made use of his power. By natural equipment, instinct, and experience, he was by far the best hunter
of the three. Keen of scent, swift of foot, and mute of
tongue, when he set nose to a scent they could be sure the
trail was a live one with a live beast at the end of it.
And so Boru came to be an indispensable member of their
forays—practically the leader.

It was a joyous time for him. He was man's companion,
not his servant, assured of food and warmth as his share of
the daily work. His liking for Edler grew as his dislike
for Simmonds deepened. But his affection did not ripen
into devotion. That, so long ago the memory was dormant,
he had given to a woman in the first flush of a young dog's

fealty, and, true to his breed, he remained faithful to his first love.

He reveled in his freedom, the crisp air, the chase, the thrill of sighting the game, the fury of the baited beast when they put up a mountain lion, his own supple alertness and perfect coördination of mind and body; leaping in to strike, out to evade the lightning parry, the taste of the hot flesh at last, and so the home trail at dusk to fire and shelter, with Edler's approving hand on his head as they went along, and perhaps the smart of an honorable wound to remind him of the joy of combat as he licked it before he stretched himself to sleep.

One morning in mid-March the trio started after fresh meat to replenish their larder. A round of their traps proved disappointing, and two hours' scouting failed to show any sign of trail that promised either fur or food. A heavy snow had been falling for two days, and it was hard work breaking trail. The men, equipped with snowshoes, taking it in turns to follow in the path trodden by the leader were better off than Boru. Boru, handicapped by his paws, sinking in the drifts, followed Edler. At times this brought him between the two men.

As the morning wore on Simmonds always surly, vented his disappointment by closing up on Boru when the wolfhound was ahead of him, striking at his hocks with the edge of the snowshoes. For a while Boru accepted this as an accident till a sharp blow sent him floundering, with an involuntary yelp of pain. Edler turned.

"What ails the dog?" he asked.

"Just plumb lazy," Simmonds answered. "No use in going farther," he went on. "Game's left the country. It's played out; we've chased 'em off."

Edler shrugged his shoulders, partly at the apparent truth that their continuous hunting over a comparatively small area had made game scarce, partly at the palpable lie at Boru's laziness, and kept on breaking trail. Simmonds followed doggedly, and, watching his chance, kicked viciously at the dog.

Boru turned with a snarl, and Simmonds threw his rifle to his hip as Edler swung about.

"You leave that dog alone!" he said.

"I'll blow his damned head off if he shows his teeth at me!" retorted Simmonds.

"If you do, you'll go out with him," said Edler. "The dog don't snarl for nothing."

The two men faced each other, Boru, between them, watching Simmonds' slightest movement. Edler's gray eyes held Simmonds' black ones in a steady challenge, and the latter's faltered.

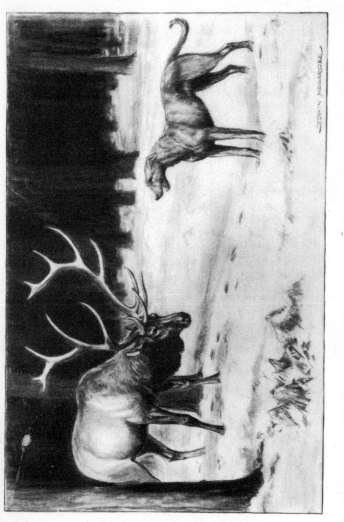

BORU LAY ON THE SNOW A LITTLE IN FRONT OF THE ELK AND WAITED PATIENTLY. HE WAS GLAD OF THE REST, THOUGH THE ELK WAS THE WEARIER OF THE TWO

"Then keep the hound out of my road," he said, and dropped the muzzle of his rifle.

He went ahead, and Boru dropped behind Edler. He had glimpsed the hate that lay in Simmonds' glance, both for himself and Edler, a hate that crouched because it feared to leap, and he strengthened his resolve to keep the former's movements under close inspection. Next time, he determined, he would not snarl, but bite and, once the issue was opened, carry it to a finish.

The action of a bull elk that sprang out from the edge of the pines that covered the ridge they were climbing, temporarily cleared the situation. The rifles went simultaneously to the men's shoulders and the bullets sped, with explosions dulled by the silencers. Masses of sensitively balanced snow fell from the trees, loosened by the shock. Simmonds' bullet roughed the crust between the legs of the startled elk as Edler's struck behind the shoulder, a little low, passing through the great body and tearing a great wound on the farther side, through which the blood poured. The elk staggered, then plunged off through the snow.

Boru started in pursuit, and the men took up the trail, made plain by scarlet splotches.

The elk galloped north, distancing Boru at first. But he followed, confident of catching up before long, gladdened by the fact that the quarry was unconsciously galloping

larderward, and resolved to keep him headed in that direction. It was hard work through the soft snow, but the
lust of the hunt offset tiredness, and he galloped on, the
men far behind.

Snow was beginning to sift down again, not enough to
obliterate tracks or disturb the scent, but threatening heavy
fall within a few hours. After a mile he could tell the
elk was slackening speed. The tracks of fore and hind
hoofs were closer together, the blood was more plentiful.
Half a mile more, and he caught sight of the wounded
animal, laboring up the opposite slope of a ridge parallel
with and close to the border line of the park.

Boru gained on the upslope as the great beast plunged on,
losing strength at every stride. At the verge of the trees,
Boru, sprang, snapping at the hocks, but the elk, with
humped back, spun about, raking at the dog with horns
that rattled against the pine stems. Boru circled and the
elk wheeled with him until it came to bay with its rump
between two trunks, safe from a flank attack, lowered head
and antlers a formidable and effective barrier.

Boru lay on the snow a little in front of the elk and waited
patiently. He was glad of the rest, though the elk was
the wearier of the two. His head hung heavily, his tongue
lolled from his jaws, and his breath smoked over the snow
in laboring puffs, while the blood spurted from his shoulder

at every shuddering heave of his body. Twice he essayed to move. Instantly Boru was up and alert, and the discouraged elk remained on wide-planted forelegs waiting for the inevitable end.

It came quickly. Two shadows fell across the snow, and Boru jumped up, with a side glance of greeting for Edler. As he rose, something, signaled instantly by sight, sound, and scent, challenged, and from his throat issued the warning he only used for human interference.

A man came striding through the trees, the carbine in his hands ready for action.

"Hands up there!" The command rang out sharply, and Simmonds and Edler obeyed.

The newcomer came up with a confident smile.

"I've got you this time," he said. "You've been having a snap of it all winter, but the jig's up. It's a long hike to camp, and we'd better be moving."

Simmonds cursed but Edler laughed at the man wearing the brass buttons of authority.

"What's eatin' you, partner?" he queried. "You ain't got nothin' on us."

The cavalryman's quizzical glance took in the wounded elk, Boru, the two men, and the rifles in the snow where they had dropped them.

"Oh, no!" he said. "I ain't got nothing on you. I saw

the dog trail the elk.   I come across lots to meet you, an'
I ain't got nothin' on you at all."

The elk stirred, and Boru sprang to face the move.

"Better call off your dog," said the soldier.   "I sure hate
to shoot him."

"You'll shoot nothin', you fool!" broke in Edler.   "Get
back where you belong."

The man stared.

"You ain't in the park by half a mile," went on Edler,
"an' you ain't got no more authority than a jack rabbit."

The soldier looked incredulous.

"Then why did you stick your hands up so prompt?" he
asked.

"Because a fool who didn't know where the line was
'u'd be likely to do most anything with a gun loose in his
hands.   Better look up your monuments, bub.   This is
Montana."

The soldier hesitated.

"You shot the elk in the park," he said.   "It's park
property."

"Who's to prove it?" jeered Simmonds.

"There's the trail."

"It won't be there in half an hour," said Edler, "way
the snow's comin' down.   Better get back to camp, sonny,
before you get lost."

THE CHIPMUNK SAT UP SUDDENLY ON A LITTLE BOULDER, ITS HEAD TO ONE SIDE, THE FRINGED TAIL CURVED ABOVE THE STRIPED BODY. THEY WERE BOTH FULL OF SPRINGTIME FROLIC. HERE WAS A GAME—A RISKY ONE, BUT A GAME FOR ALL OF THAT

The soldier flushed angrily under his tan. He had made a false move, and he knew it.

"If I ever get you on the right side of the line, look out!" he said angrily. "And if that dog of yours comes my way, it won't be elk blood they'll find on the snow."

"Talk's cheap," said Edler. "Good-by, soldier."

The patrolman turned and went down the hill on his skis. The thickening snow shut him out of sight.

A groan came from the wounded elk. Its knees gave way, and it fell on the snow. Boru leaped, too late for the kill. The big head tried to lift, then fell back with dull eyes, its antlers half buried in the snow.

"Out of the way, Buck," said Edler, taking his knife from its sheath. "We got to hurry. It's goin' to snow hard."

Boru lay down, his mouth watering at the thought of the share soon to be thrown to him. Simmonds stood still, not offering to help Edler cut up the dead elk.

"Nice mess the dog's got us into now," he said. "Now they've got us spotted for fair."

Edler did not answer, but went on with his work of deftly skinning the carcass.

An ugly look crept into Simmonds' eyes. He turned slowly and intercepted Boru's persistent gaze. There was something shining in the dog's glance that he could not meet—suspicion, hatred, purpose, and, back of it all, knowledge.

"Damned if I don't think that brute can think!" he muttered. "I'll have to get rid of him."

And Boru, forgetful of the meat, still watching him, accepted the challenge.

CHAPTER FIVE

LOVE AND HOME

It was the end of June in the Yellowstone National Park. Winter is long and the snow lies late six thousand feet above sea level, so that Summer overtakes the lazy Spring before the latter is well started on her tasks, and the two conclude them hand in hand. The wild roses were out and the land gay with blooms; the cottonwoods were screened in new green, and the cedars showed vivid tippings of their darker foliage. Everywhere the sap was mounting, buds unfolding, birds and beasts mating, the ferment of life rioting in tissues animate and inanimate.

Among the dappled shadows of a thicket that bordered a fast-flowing stream, glacier-fed, trout-filled, Boru frolicked like a puppy of six weeks, rather than the wolfhound of six years' varied experience that he was. High on a palisaded crest a fish eagle looked down on him with supercilious contempt. Prone behind a bush, his hind legs crouched ready for a leap, his gray coat checkered to invisibility, Boru, his ears at half cock, watched the gambols of a chipmunk, frisking, unsuspicious and carefree, almost within reach of a bound.

Boru did not want the chipmunk for purposes of provender. He hardly expected to catch it after the experience of a score of similar attempts, all unsuccessful. It was the spring in his veins, the delicious madness that for some brief hours swings back the shadow on the dial for beast and man alike and makes us young again. So he pretended, for the sheer pleasure of the play, that the chipmunk, about half as large as his own ear, was a bear of mammoth proportions, far greater than the maker of the fresh slot he had crossed that morning. In a moment, he would charge and annihilate it.

The chipmunk sat up suddenly on a little bowlder, its head to one side, the fringed tail curved above the striped body. One beady bright eye looked in Boru's direction. The wolfhound sprang, launched high in air from the urge of his powerful loins—fifteen feet from his crouch, his forepaws landing close together on the stone whence the chipmunk had vanished with a flicker of fur and a whisk of plumed, indignant tail.

The chipmunk clung halfway up an aspen, peering round the trunk and scolding vigorously while Boru looked up with a foolish, good-natured grin. Perhaps the squirrel had been playing, too. The attitude of one clinging claw and the tone of its *cha! cha! cha!* were wonderfully suggestive of an urchin with fingers to nose and taunt of "couldn't catch me."

Boru tried to look as if he hadn't meant the leap, and ignored the squirrel's mocking chatter. Then he turned his attention to some broad-bladed grass that he loved to nip and chew, snapped at the flying grasshoppers, and strolled down to lap the cold, swift water of the stream.

He was in perfect fettle, in far better condition than when he had captured the trophies for winner in all his classes, "best of his breed" and "best dog in the show," three years before, at Madison Square Garden; the best Irish wolfhound ever bred in or imported to America. Beneath his glossy coat of crisp, wavy gray-brindle hair, the muscles played about his limbs and lean ribs, unhampered by an extra ounce of flesh. His dark-brown eyes were lustrous; he stood well up on his pads, a hundred and ninety pounds of concentrated energy, just short of forty inches in height at the shoulders. The triumphs of his show days were a lost issue, the memory of his mistress, the only human being he had ever loved with that mysterious tie between the human and the canine soul, was an emotion long submerged. All his by-days—the kennels of his puppyhood, the vaudeville act in which he had figured, the circus from which he had escaped to the wild, his whelps, even his dead mate, the white wolf—all were forgotten in the sheer joy of present living.

A man came up the stream, wading knee-deep, deftly casting a grasshopper-baited line into likely-looking eddies and riffles. As Boru watched, crouching in the grass, the line tautened, the rod bent as the tip went up, and, after a short, gallant fight, a trout flapped gasping in the shallows and the man grasped it by the gills.

"Hello, Buck," said the fisherman, as Boru stood up, his tail wagging in friendly recognition. "Fish for dinner. This makes the dozen. Come on, let's go home."

Boru thrust his muzzle against the man's palm, in token of comradeship, not servitude, and sniffed at the plump rainbows strung on a willow withe. He liked Edler, almost as strongly as he disliked Edler's cabin mate, Simmonds. He liked fish, too, particularly after Edler had cooked them and they had cooled off, and he knew his share would be forthcoming in payment for his work as general guardian and fellow huntsman to the camp to which he had attached himself. So he trotted along in his friend's trail, contentedly licking his chops in anticipation of his meal.

Simmonds sat on a stump outside the cabin, smoking. He looked up as Edler came up with Boru.

"Good luck?" he queried. Edler paused, surprised at the evident attempt at friendliness in the tone. Six months at close quarters between two opposite natures had not endeared the men to each other. However, if Simmonds elected to break his sulky silence, Edler saw no reason to reject the overture. But Boru passed into the cabin, ignoring Simmonds as if he had been a part of the stump he sat upon.

"All we can eat," replied Edler, holding up his string. "They're thicker'n flies. Ready for grub?"

"In a minnit," replied Simmonds. "Set down the fish where that damned dog won't get 'em. I've got a scheme to put up to ye."

"The dog won't touch 'em. You know that."

Simmonds grunted. Edler went into the cabin and came out, pipe in mouth.

"What's the proposition?" he asked, lighting up and speaking between puffs. "Any money in it?"

Boru came to the door of the shack and stretched himself along the threshold, his nose between his paws, his eyes watching the two men as they talked. He noted the new friendliness in the two voices and wondered at it as he listened. His vocabulary was not a large one, but he was a master of tone and, with his senses sharpened by liking for Edler and distrust of Simmonds, bred from the latter's treatment of him, he followed the trend of the talk far more closely than either of the men could have imagined possible.

Simmonds was discussing him, he knew, as certainly as if the man's language was his own, and he watched him keenly beneath his shaggy brows.

"Money?" echoed Simmonds. "That's what we're *both* needin', ain't it? That cur you take such a shine to queered it for us since we had the run-in with the patrol."

"It wasn't his fault the yellow leg spotted him trailin' the elk," said Edler.

"Well, they've got *us* spotted, all right," grumbled Simmonds. "There's no doin' anything, the way they keep tabs on this end of the park. We've got to move, and it takes money. You seem to like the place lately," he added, with a sneer.

Edler flushed, and covered it by lighting an unnecessary match.

"I'm through with the poachin' game, I told you that last week," he said.

"Yah!" Simmonds spat viciously on the ground. "That sounds like woman's talk. But there's nothing in the way things stand, an' the prices that old miser Higgins puts on skins. But there's something in what I'm goin' to put up to you."

He got up and glanced cautiously about the little clearing. Then he joined Edler on the fallen log, where the latter had seated himself.

"It's open season for tourists," he said, in a low tone. "Hotels all opened up. It costs a heap of money to live at them places. They ain't no banks here. The tourists tote it with 'em, an', when they make the stage tours, they natcherally packs it with 'em."

He paused, covertly watching the effect of his words on Edler, who said nothing but knocked out the ashes of his pipe on the log and refilled it. Boru could sense his displeasure, but Simmonds' intuitions were duller, and he edged closer and went on confidentially, elbows on knees.

"It ain't the first time it's been done," he said. "An' it won't be the last. It's a snap. All one way, an' no come back. They'se no guard on the stages, they ain't got no military escort, an' *they don't allow no weapons in the park.*" He grinned as he emphasized the last sentence. "Why it'll be like takin' pie from a picnic party."

Edler looked at him evenly.

"Thinkin' of holdin' up a stage?" he asked.

"I've got it all doped out," Simmonds continued, tapping his companion's knee for emphasis. Edler shifted his position, crossing his legs to avoid the touch. Simmonds went on, unnoting the movement.

"Listen. The down stage leaves Mammoth Hot Springs at eight to-morrow mornin' an' hits Norris for lunch. They stop at Obsidian Cliff midway about ten. There's the place to tag 'em. We'll start after lunch, cross the river at New Bridge, follow down Lowe Crick, cross Lava Crick forks, an' camp out at Lake of the Woods. In the mornin', we'll lay among the bowlders, head of Beaver Lake, west side of the road. They stop at the Glass Cliff to rubber an' listen to the driver blat his line of talk. While they're all ears an' eyes, we steps out an' covers 'em.

"We'll empty the gas tank, mebbe shoot the tires flat, *sabe?* An' we'll tie up the bunch good an' make our sneak across Straight Crick an' Indian Crick ranges. We can work out gradual through Bighorn Pass or Fawn Pass an' hit the G. an' P. for a freight.

"It's simple as falling off a log. There's bound to be a good haul an' no risk."

"That's what recommends it to you, likely," said Edler drily, as he rose from the log.

Boru got up, too. There was trouble in the air, and he knew which side he was going to take if it became necessary. Habitually he treated Simmonds with a tolerant contempt that, in a man, would have spelled fight, but beneath it all was a very real and living hatred that only lacked provocative action on the part of Simmonds, to break out in an attempt to even many old scores.

"Well, what d'ye say?"

Edler looked down at the other man with a direct gaze, before which Simmonds' eyes shifted.

"Just this," he said; "I've been outside the law, with you, all winter, poaching on gov'ment preserves. I've had my own theories about gov'ment right to coax in an' coop all the game. Mebbe I was wrong—mebbe right. But there's a whole heap of difference in playing the game against an armed patrol that's hired to keep you out, an' jumpin' out on a lot of scared tourists without a pea shooter to protect the bunch of 'em."

"Yah!" repeated Simmonds, and spat again, to express his contempt.

"What's more," Edler went on; "there *is* a risk. We'll be suspected, first thing, an' we'll have four troops of cavalry out after us, mounted. I'll have nothing to do with it."

"Then I'll do it on my own hook."

"No, you won't."

Simmonds got up and faced Edler, his face working angrily, flushed beneath its swarthy tan. Boru came out of the cabin doorway and moved halfway toward the two men.

"I won't, eh?" sneered Simmonds. "An' who's goin' to stop me?"

"I am," replied Edler quietly. "You're identified with

me, an' you ain't goin' to drag me into any mess you're fool enough to get yourself into."

"Afraid, eh?" Simmonds laughed, his stained teeth showing through his beard. "I though mebbe you'd jest turned mushy moral 'count of thet gal of Higgins you've been courtin' down to Deevers. You can go sparkin' her an' prove an alibi if you want to."

Through a long winter Edler had heaped up a high pile of the fuel of resentment against his selfish, surly partner. The mention of the girl's name was the match, and the flame leaped high, its light gleaming in Edler's gray eyes.

"You'll keep her name out of your dirty mouth," he said; "an' you'll get your traps out of my shack an' keep clear o' this neck o' the woods."

"The woods is free, I reckon."

"There ain't room in this section for both of us," returned Edler. "I was here first. You came in at my asking. Now you can go on my asking, an' you can't go none too soon to suit me."

He swung on his heel and turned to enter the cabin. The red spark of hate in his eyes was matched by the glare in Simmonds' before the latter's lids narrowed over the glittering black orbs and bloodshot whites. His right hand dropped to his belt, where his hunting knife swung in its sheath. With an oath, he jerked out the gleaming blade and sprang to drive it between the shoulder blades of the man who had turned back on him.

Fast as he moved, Boru was swifter. The moment he had been expecting had come, and he was ready for it. The deep growl in his throat echoed Simmonds' oath, and his leap forestalled the man's stride. Edler saw him gather for the leap, and, guessing what was up, whirled.

In mid-air, Boru's teeth had closed on Simmonds' wrist with a vicious grip that sent the knife tinkling to the ground, while the weight of the wolfhound's lunging body set the man asprawl, trying to protect himself from the dog's attack at his throat.

Edler locked his arms around Boru's chest and tried to pull him off. For the first time, Boru snarled at his friend. He had attacked in Edler's protection; but, in a way, it had been only an excuse for his own fight. His blood was up and his foe was down. The stings of a hundred insults urged him to finish it.

Panting and tugging, Edler managed to haul Boru off and hold him in his arms for a moment. Boru struggled violently, a continuous snarl gurgling in his throat, but he did not attempt to bite Edler. Simmonds scrambled to all fours, his face pallid with fear and wet with sweat.

"Run for the cabin, you fool!" cried Edler. "I can't hold him."

With a sudden, twisting surge of all his muscles, Boru broke loose and sprang for the fleeing man, who reached the shack just in time to slam the door against the plunging paws. Boru reared against the barrier, leaped back and launched himself in a living battering-ram. Then he realized the futility of trying to break through, and stood back, expending his wrath in deep—throated barks.

"Let him go, Buck," said Edler. "He ain't worth it."

He went to the side of the cabin where the window was and called out to Simmonds.

"I'm goin' to take the dog out of the way for an hour," he said. "In the meantime you can clear out, you back-knifing skunk."

There was no answer, and Edler returned to where Boru, his barking spent, lay couched in front of the door, waiting for his enemy to emerge.

"Come on, Buck," said Edler. "Best thing to do is to get shut of him, the murderin' swine."

Boru looked at him reluctantly. Edler moved off to the edge of the timber, coaxing him. Boru's anger had evaporated somewhat. After all, he had knocked his enemy down. He wished he had crunched harder on that wrist. Still, if Edler insisted upon it, now that Simmonds was out of reach—the matter could be put off. He rose and trotted slowly after his friend.

Half a mile into the woods, Edler halted and sat down on a stump. Boru stopped and looked at him questioningly as he slapped his knee and laughed.

"Darned if it ain't a joke on us, Buck," he said. "He's got the best of us. Blamed if I didn't leave the trout in the shack. Here's where we lose our lunch. I can smoke," he added, taking out his pipe. "What are *you* going to do about it?"

Boru yawned. His philosophy was equal to Edler's tobacco. Hunger meant little to him these days. With a half turn in the fern, he dropped to the ground with a sigh, stretching himself, cocked one eye at Edler lighting his pipe, then closed both of them and went to sleep.

When Edler and Boru got back to the cabin, the door was open and the place empty. Edler had improvised a lead for Boru from his belt, with his neckerchief for collar, fearful that Simmonds might attempt to shoot the dog if he appeared first and unprotected. But there was no occasion for the precaution. Simmonds had departed, taking his belongings with him.

Edler gave his attention to the pile of skins which lay tumbled on the floor where Simmonds had selected his share, and was congratulating himself on the apparent fairness of division, when Boru distracted his attention.

Boru had a definite idea that his enemy had made a final

departure, but the scent of the man, which was unpleasant in his nostrils, still haunted the cabin, and was indeed, so strong for an absentee that he doubted his sense and went sniffing suspiciously about the cabin. At a point by the rough table, he halted and growled.

"What is it Buck?" Edler crossed the floor and looked at the objects Boru was nosing. Then he stooped and picked them up, two roughly circular pieces of black silk about the size of a half dollar.

Edler whistled softly. "Cut out of *my* black scarf, darn his hide!" he said. "He's made a mask of it. He's goin' to tackle that stage to-morrow mornin' alone. I didn't think he had the nerve, spite of there bein' no chance of a scrap. We've got to stop him, Buck. They'll catch him, sure, an' we'll get mixed up in it. They've got us listed at the fort for suspicious characters long ago. He'll never get clear. We've got to stop him."

Boru looked up at Edler with a gaze that told his readiness and knowledge of the work in hand.

Edler reflected. He might take the road that ran from Yancy's to the fort and warn them of the contemplated holdup. But the explanation that would be insisted upon would more or less involve him in the matter, and he was particularly anxious to keep a clear record for himself, and let any suspicions that might be held against him at the fort die down.   Simmonds had hit the mark with his mention of the daughter of Higgins, the trader at Deevers.   It was for her sake Edler had made up his mind to foreswear dubious methods of making a living and take up some ranch land close to the railroad.

"We'll try to trail him, Buck," he said, "an' do a little holding up ourselves.   More'n likely he'll work it out as he planned.   He'll have to cross the river at new Bridge anyways.   You an' me'll grub up, Buck, an' hit the trail.   It'll be up to you mostly.   We'll have to keep goin', an' I'll be no good trailin' by moonlight."

Boru wagged his tail and waited impatiently until Edler was ready.   The latter took apart his rifle and disposed of it in a blanket pack that carried food for the trip, and slipped a magazine load of cartridges into his pocket.

The two started on their long hike two hours after noon.   Boru picked up the trail from the cabin door, but Edler called him off.

"We'll keep your nose till later, Buck," he said, "and cut across lots for the bridge."

Boru acquiesced.   He had a lot of confidence in Edler, who talked to him as if he had been another man by the name of Buck.

The title of Buck suited Boru's taste.   He had almost forgotten that he had ever had any other name, and he ac-

cepted Edler's impromptu.   Through close association, he
was keenly alive to Edler's moods and the tone sense of
what he said, and he fully comprehended that the expedi-
tion had the finding of Simmonds for its objective.   He
knew, moreover, that the mission was not a friendly one,
and that also satisfied him.   If, at the end of the trail, the
opportunity came for him to settle his quarrel with Simmonds, well and good.   For the moment he was content in
present action, with Edler, who evidently knew what he
was about, in the lead.

The chief hunting ally of a wolfhound is its sight.
Trained for generations to run with the quarry in full view,
the original quality of nose has depreciated, although in in-
dividuals it is sometimes well developed.   Boru's year in the
wilds had brought his capacity for catching and holding a
scent almost up to that of his one-time mate, the wolf's.
This and his powers of observation worked hand in hand.
And the scent of a man was peculiarly pungent and distinguishable.   The wolf-dog tribe, Irish and Russian alike,
recognize human friends after an absence through the nose
rather than eyes but to follow Simmonds' comparatively
fresh trail as soon as Edler gave him the word, was not going to be a difficult task.

They made the eight miles to the bridge across the Yellowstone in less than three hours, and followed the road south to Lower Falls, leaving it there for the trail down Lower Creek. The way led along the foot of high cliffs, the only practical mode of travel, and there Edler turned over the leadership to Boru.

"If you can pick up the trail here, Buck," he said, "it's tolerably certain he's gone through to Lake of the Woods. We may not catch up ter night; he's got two hours start of us, an' we're trailin', but we'll get him to-morrer, an' put a joker in his deck. Good dog."

Boru did not need the aid of the discarded neckerchief of Simmonds that Edler held to his nose. He caught the odor that was so repugnant to him with its reek of enmity arousing subconsciously the emotion of rage and, with a look backward, went rapidly down the trail at a trot that kept Edler between a walk and a run to keep him in sight. At Carnelian Creek he was fairly blown and called a halt. Boru lay down beside him while he rested, wondering at the delay and at the weakness of the man whom he acknowledged superior in so many things.

"I'll have to leash you up, Buck," Edler said, "or you'll be losing me."

Boru submitted, and they went on. At the next creek coming in from the south they had to cross the stream, but picked up the trail again. It was dusk; Edler made a fire and produced camp bread and beans liberally larded with bacon, also coffee in an old pot. These, except the last, Boru shared, then got up and followed the trail a little way, going back to Edler and looking at him impatiently. He was a dog of one purpose, and when he concentrated upon it, followed it out without regard to fatigue and obstacle.

"Moon'll be up in about an hour, Buck," said Edler, lighting his pipe, "I ain't got night eyes, like you have. I'd break my neck follerin' ye. Take a rest. Too bad you can't smoke."

Boru subsided under the force of circumstances, bound by his companion's limitations, and waited, passing the time in light dog naps till the full moon shone down the cañon and Edler took up his pack.

Yard by yard, mile by mile, Boru, his neck hard into the improvised collar, led the way. Besides his unerring nose, his night eyes saw a hundred signs that Edler missed, could not, indeed, have distinguished in the daytime. The displaced pebbles where a heavy foot had stepped, rank with the individual odor of the man they tracked, the dottel of a pipe where Simmonds had knocked it out against a tree and, close on to midnight, the ashes and half-burned boughs of a fire where he had stopped for supper.

They crossed the plateau beyond Lower Creek, Storm Peak and Observation Peak, lifting high to right and left, like sentinels, and, at two in the morning, made a night camp between the extreme western forks of Lava Creek, five miles from the tiny Lake of the Woods where Simmonds was presumably spending the night. Edler was worn out and frankly admitted it to Boru, who was tired, too, but would have kept on. But the moon was sinking behind the bulk of Handmark Mountain, and progress was difficult through the rough country. Edler had already stumbled and barely saved himself from serious injury, and he feared a sprained ankle in the coming darkness.

"We can make it in two hours in the morning, Buck," he said. "We'll turn in till sunup. If you wake first, call me."

He rolled up in his blanket, and was snoring in two minutes. Boru dozed until the first rays of the sun rimmed Handmark with crimson, then he went to Edler and nosed his face with his cold muzzle.

Edler sat up, yawning, and stretched himself.

"Reglar old alarm clock, ain't ye?" he asked, scratching Boru behind the ears. "Right on the dot. Let's eat."

It seemed certain that Simmonds was carrying out his program, and Edler debated taking a crosscut direct to Obsidian Cliff, but decided upon the safer course.

"He may have changed his mind at the last minute, Buck," he said. "We'll keep the trail."

He adjusted the lead and collar and, before the sun had chased the shadows to the base of the peaks, Boru had found the scent again. He led the way unerringly to the warm ashes of Simmonds' fire by the little lake and thence to the regular trail that led to the stage road half a mile below Beaver Lake. The way was marshy and the imprints of heavy shoes showed here and there. Edler recognized them by their contour and the placing of the nails; Boru knew them by sight and the scent they held, and they pressed on.

Where the trail reached the stage road and ended, they saw the footprints leading plain across the dusty highway. Edler looked at his watch.

"You an' me'll go along the cliffs, Buck," he said. "Time we get to Obsidian, Simmonds'll be taking position. We can stop him easy from the bluff. It'd be hard work getting the drop on him from behind, the cover's too slim, an' he'd see us if we come along the road."

They kept along the cliffs that bordered the eastern side of the road and looked down upon Beaver Lake, that paralleled it on the opposite side, keeping back from the edge, making quick progress over the flinty rock. Opposite the head of the lake, where Obsidian Creek issued on to a willowy flat, there was a notch in the edge of the cliff, split deeply into the volcanic glass and commanding a good view of the stage road and the bowlders among which Simmonds had planned to set up his ambush. They settled themselves as best they could, and Edler swept the lake with his glasses.

There was no sign of Simmonds. From their superior height, it was impossible for him to escape their notice, and Edler began to curse softly.

"We should have kept on his trail, Buck," he said to Boru, perched uncomfortably on the hard rock, supporting himself upright by forelegs set against one side of the slope.

Boru, his red tongue hanging out, perspiration dripping from its end, ceased his survey and turned his eyes to Edler. There was reassurance in them. It was almost as if he nodded.

"Think he's there, do you?" asked Edler. "Mebbe you see something I can't, or smell something."

Boru blinked. It was his mode of assent. Edler looked at his watch again. It was a quarter past eight. Then he hit his knee with a satisfied slap and grinned. Simmonds' watch was thirty minutes slower than his, he remembered. They had had a controversy about it. He was sure his own was right.

"He thinks he's got over two hours, Buck," he said. "He's taking his time."

Boru blinked again in superior wisdom. He had seen and smelled something that had escaped Edler. His keen eyes had noted a series of tiny smoke threads from the willows a quarter of a mile away, and the wind brought with it a whiff of burning tobacco, too faint for the man's apprehension. Boru knew as well as if he had seen him that Simmonds was in the willows, smoking. He looked round. Edler had taken his rifle from his pack, and was getting it in readiness for action. The man had taken the lead again, and Boru, knowing well the uses of the weapon, acquiesced. His animosity was not at that moment active enough against Simmonds for him to dispute Edler's handling of the affair. But he watched intently, anticipating a shot. Then, as happened often with the four-footed game they hunted, if the quarry was only wounded, he would rush in and finish.

Edler methodically filled the magazine with the cartridges from his pocket. Contrary to Boru's thought, he had no fixed expectation of using them, but he was prepared for trouble. He took out his pipe and then put it back reluctantly.

The minutes passed, marked by the tick of the watch Edler had set beside him and the march of the shadows down one slope of the notch. The hands slipped around the dial until they showed at half-past nine. By Simmonds' time it would be nine. Edler looked up the road toward Apollinaris Springs. The stage was likely to appear any moment now. He shifted anxiously in his seat. Boru sat imperturbable. The tobacco smell had passed, but every now and then a whiff of human odor told him Simmonds was still in the willows.

Suddenly he stood up, bracing himself, and turned his head to Edler, his eyes eager. He had sighted a movement in the boughs that was not wind. Edler took up his glasses. Simmonds, his rifle at trail, was coming out of the low trees.

Clear of them, he looked about him, then cautiously crept from bowlder to bowlder. Up the straight road, Edler could see the dust of the stage. It would be opposite them in fifteen minutes.

Simmonds was coming forward more rapidly, gliding from rock to rock like a lizard. At last he halted between two bowlders, close to the edge of the road, two hundred feet away from the watchers. Edler set hand on Boru's neck, but the wolfhound had entered into the spirit of the double ambuscade, and sat, save for his quivering tongue and shining eyes, like a statue of gray stone.

Simmonds' face, covered with the sinister black mask, peered out from between the rocks and looked up the road. The stage was in sight now. The scene was set. In two minutes the curtain would be raised.

Simmonds squatted back like a great toad, cuddling his

rifle, waiting for the auto stage to make its customary stop. Edler slid forward his rifle, knelt, rested the weapon on a rock, and drew a bead on the wouldbe bandit. Then he called across the road:

"Drop that rifle, Simmonds. Drop it! Now get back a bit. Slow. Stop where you are! I ain't goin' to give you away, but if you make a move, I'll plug you."

Simmonds looked up at the voice, his evil eyes glittering through the holes in the mask. He couldn't see Edler, but he saw Boru's head watching him and, beside it, his straining vision made out the muzzle of a rifle ending in a Maxim silencer. A little brush that grew between the bowlders half hid him as he crept obediently back. Amid the growth and the shadow, he was hardly distinguishable, save from Edler's superior angle of sight. From the road or the coach top he was invisible, screened by the rocks between him and the highway.

Boru sat still except for the tremors that twitched beneath his rough coat, waiting for the shot, intent upon Simmonds, unconscious of the stage. Edler, holding his rifle, looking through the circle of his telescopic sight, temporarily forgot him.

The stage braked. The driver, turning half round, proclaimed his invariable description.

"This cliff," he announced, "is made of solid glass,

obsidyun, of volcanic formation, used by the Indians for arrerheads. Ol' Jim Bridger used ter tell erbout it an' folks thought he lied, but there 'tis. The road is the only glass road in the world, made by buildin' fires agin' the cliff an' splashin' cold water to split out the chunks."

There was a chorus of "oh's" and "ah's" from the passengers, unconscious of the elements of excitement and tragedy so close at hand. Edler's rifle remained motionless and menacing. Boru, hidden from the stage by the height of the cliff, was still at frozen gaze and, in his ambush, Simmonds, deprived of his weapon, gritted his teeth and crouched.

The driver released his brake and shifted to second as the big car rolled on. Suddenly Edler missed Boru, but he did not move from his covering of Simmonds.

As the stage came opposite the cleft it attracted Boru's attention. A puff of wind slanted upward, bearing a scent that thrilled and confused him. There was the odor of gasoline fumes, but there was something else, a persistent, a pleasant essence. The blood rushed to his head, a hundred thoughts seemed pounding in his brain for admission to conscious expression. Impelled by some strange force, he bounded up the steep sides of the cliff and stood on the edge, looking down on the stage, his nostrils distended.

"Hey, look at that gray wolf!" cried one of the passengers. The rest craned their necks to see.

"All kinds of wild animals in the park," said the driver, without braking.

But Boru was gazing wildly at the figure of a girl in a linen duster, half starting from the seat.

"That's not a wolf," she said. "That's an Irish wolfhound. I owned one once. Father, look! Do you suppose that could be Boru?"

The stout man beside her laughed, and she sat back, turning her neck as the stage rolled on up the stiff grade, to look back at Boru. He trotted along the cliff, whining, looked over the precipitous edge uncertainly, still in the maze of thoughts that would not quicken to understanding, and watched the big car until it disappeared around a curve. Puzzled, he trotted slowly back to where Edler now stood in the cleft, addressing Simmonds.

"Git up an' git!" he called. "Stick up yore hands and go over to them willers. Then keep goin'. Never mind yore gun. You better clear from the park, because I'm goin' to tip off the fort."

Simmonds snarled viciously at the threat, not knowing that Edler bluffed, held up his hands, and retreated sullenly to the willows. When he had gone, Edler, followed by Boru, clambered down the cleft and made his way to the road, his rifle ready for action.

Simmonds had vanished. Edler picked up his weapon.

"I'll swop this for the silk handkerchief he took," he said with a laugh. "Come on, Buck, we'll be gettin' back. I got a date to-night. We can make it if we hump ourselves. No use in followin' up that skunk."

But Boru, in the whirl of emotions, had forgotten Simmonds. He was snuffing in the trail of the stage, trying to secure a repetition of the strangely familiar scent that had raised the ferment in his brain, trying hard to rouse disused cells to action—to remember.

Alone in the cabin that night, with Edler gone to Deevers to keep his appointment with Higgins' daughter, memory leaped suddenly alive. The odor that had prevailed over the conflicting scents from the stage was the odor of his beloved, of his mistress of long ago, to whom his heart still held fealty. The ache in his heart for the touch of her hand and the sound of her voice calling to him grew intolerable, and he leaped to his feet, eager to retrace the long journey to the cliff, and from there seek her out. His tired limbs grew supple, and his heart pounded.

He jumped to his feet and sought for an exit. The door

was closed and, try as he would, he could not open it. Whining, he ran round the room. The stars looked in at the little window between the balsam boughs.

Boru backed, measured his distance, his muscles tautened to steel wires. From the center of the floor he leaped.

Edler, coming home after midnight, tired out, on a borrowed horse, found the window frame carried away, the glass broken and shattered, and the cabin empty.

"I'll be darned!" he said. "I wonder what ailed the dog? Mountain lion, mebbe. Well," he yawned sleepily, "he'll be back in the mornin', I reckon."

But Boru was racing down the trail by Lower Creek on worn pads that were urged to fleetness by the desire of his heart, bound by the tie that does not gall, the undying love of a dog for the one he chooses to call master or mistress.

The northern boundary of the Yellowstone National Park crosses Electric Peak, over eleven thousand feet high, the tallest crest of the region. A range of foothills, in which Gardiner River rises, is separated from the main peak by a saddle, north of which the mountain lifts rapidly.

On the saddle, stretched on a rocky ledge, shaded from the morning sun, Boru lay, moody and disconsolate. Two weeks of fruitless search had passed since the night he had leaped through the cabin window to find his mistress. For several days he had watched the stage pass by Obsidian Cliff, hoping once more to catch the perfume of her presence, the tone of her voice, and he had roamed many a league of road and trail, until his spirit grew morose from disappointment. Though hope had shrunk, his determination remained set. Every thought and action centered upon regaining his place by her side. Old memories, once prompted, came easily to him, and he remembered the home kennels, days when he had raced by the side of his mistress mounted upon a horse, which also had been his friend. Long walks together, caresses and dainties from her hand, standing proudly in the judging ring, while people applauded, and the man who had been looking at him and handling him so much gave his mistress something that he had won. All the devotion that a dog loves to lavish upon the object of his affections, worthy or unworthy, welled unrestrained in his breast and filled him with a longing that was pain.

He hunted automatically and ate mechanically, resting only from sheer weariness and footsoreness, resting then in body only, not in spirit. Edler and the cabin, his feud with Simmonds, were forgotten. He lived for one end.

Save when he slept, his inactive moments were spent on some high place like the saddle of Electric Peak, where his eye could roam over long distances in the perpetual hope of seeing a figure that might turn out to be his best beloved.

He was very tired and very thin. He had only eaten when hunger grew urgent enough to clamor above the call of his heart. Then he would trail and chase and kill with a savage ferocity, that gave woodchuck, grouse, or rabbit small chance to realize their peril before it was upon them. The fortnight of hard travel, coupled with continous disappointment, had told upon him heavily; but, aside from pads worn to the quick, he was still in the prime of muscular energy. The fever of his search shone in his overbright eyes, through which looked invincible purpose.

Far down the slopes he saw two figures, mere dots against the gray rocks, toiling slowly upward. His raw pads were very tender, and as long as the figures moved toward him, he was content to lie and watch them. Presently the dots disappeared, to show again on a nearer ridge as the forms of a man and woman, mounting steadily. Boru sank his nose between his forepaws and watched them steadily. His heartbeats quickened a little as he noted the skirts of the woman, but there were many tourists in the park, and he had been foiled so often that he let his weariness offset hope until the climbers' own efforts should bring them nearer.

There had been tales told in the park hotels of a great

SAVE WHEN HE SLEPT, BORU'S INACTIVE MOMENTS WERE
SPENT ON SOME HIGH PLACE WHERE HIS EYES COULD ROAM
OVER WIDE DISTANCES IN THE PERPETUAL HOPE OF SEEING A
FIGURE THAT MIGHT TURN OUT TO BE HIS BEST BELOVED

gray wolf—that had suddenly appeared beside the trail or above it, always to a woman; and, before they could fully glimpse it in their surprise or fright, had wheeled and gone off at a swift lope.

At the Mammoth Hot Springs Hotel, only eight miles from where Boru lay crouched, Nora Manners had heard the story that morning as she stood on the veranda beside her father's chair.

It must be the big dog we saw at Obsidian Cliff, father," she declared. "The one that looked like Boru, you remember."

"A wolf, my dear."

"It was not a wolf, father. I saw the ears distinctly. I know you think I'm silly, but I can't help the feeling that it is Boru. If it should be! I've always been sorry I sold him when we broke up the kennels."

"Well, my dear," said Mr. Manners good-humoredly, "maybe you'll come across him yourself. We've three more days here, and the clerk says that he was seen over at Boiling River, close by here. Are you going to tackle that mountain this morning?"

The girl nodded.

"I talked to a man yesterday who says he knows the way to the top, and there's a wonderful view. He ought to be here any minute."

"That's the peak?"

"No, that's Sepulcher Mountain. Only a hill, father. Nine thousand feet, and we're six now. Electric Peak is worth while."

"Well, don't play yourself out. This altitude is tiring." Mr. Manners sat back in his chair and lit a cigar.

"You're lazy, dad. There's my guide now. I'll get the lunch and my alpenstock. We'll be back before dark. You won't be lonesome?"

"No. I'm going over to the fort. Good-by."

Simmonds stood outside the hotel, waiting for his employer, Edler would hardly have recognized him. He had shaved off beard and mustaches and, since the sun had tanned the long-hidden skin, was good looking in a coarse way, save for the furtive eyes and sensual mouth.

Simmonds was in an uncomfortable position. He had not dared to offer his skins for sale to Higgins, and he knew no other trader who would handle the illegal traffic. So he had cached them for the time being and, driven by lack of money and provisions, had hung around Gardiner, at the entrance to the park, doing odd jobs for his meals and borrowing a razor at the first opportunity. Hearing no reports of threatened holdups or suspicious characters, he gradually shed his fears of Edler carrying out his threat of warning the fort, and ventured to Mammoth Hot Springs under the very nose of the soldiery, offering his services as guide, cook, and general aid to picnic parties, picking up a precarious living and a few dollars.

He had three desires: To get even with Edler, to kill Boru, and to get away from the park. He had no definite plans of achieving the two first, and the last needed more money that he was likely to get hold of for a long while.

It was the big diamond on the left hand of Nora Manners that aroused his cupidity. With the price of that, he thought, he could get clear away, back to the cities. His dull brain filled with hazy ideas of a general debauch, but he dismissed them with a sigh. There was small chance of his getting the diamond. He was desperate enough to rob the hotel, but too much of a coward to accept a risk, much less such a handicap as the neighborhood of a troop of cavalry.

His surprise was as great as his satisfaction when the girl approached him, trim in her mountain clothes.

"They tell me you know the country," she said. "I want to climb Electric Peak. Can you guide me?"

"I know all the country, miss," he had answered, his eyes traveling covertly over the lithe curving figure and resting on the diamond. "I can take ye up easy."

Simmonds had never set foot on the peak, but he reckoned on his mountaineering skill to achieve the feat, and the germ of a dastardly thought had already come into his mind.

"Can we go to-morrow morning?"

"Yes, miss."

"Nine o'clock, then. Is there anything else?" she asked, as Simmonds hesitated.

"Well, you see, miss, beggin' your pardon, there's them as changes their minds an' leaves us out of a job. So it's usual——"

"Oh, I haven't any money with me! Come up to the hotel."

Simmonds, with five dollars in his pocket, laid out part of his wealth on whisky. It inflamed his dreams with crude plans of abduction and of ransom, of a beautiful girl kept captive on a high peak. Some of these were still in the fuddled web of his brain when he awoke. He bought another flask of hooch for the trip.

His practiced eye had picked the saddle ridge as the best approach to the peak, and they made good progress. The hot sun improved neither his headache nor his temper, and several times he drank from the flask, unobserved by the girl. He began to formulate the scheme as his false courage mounted with the lowering of the liquor.

The girl climbed easily, with athletic grace and skill that

brought clumsy compliments from her guide. These she ignored lightly, passing them off with questions.

"Have you heard or seen anything of a big gray wolf or dog that shows himself and then runs away?" she asked.

"Not me, miss," answered Simmonds, hardly taking in the sense of her words as he watched her standing on the brink of the cliff, the breeze whipping the loose strands of her fair hair and outlining the beauty of her figure. Women had been the bane of Simmonds' life, and he of theirs. The light in his eyes was not pleasant to look at. He had no thought of Boru. But five hundred feet above them Boru lay on his ledge waiting for them to come near enough for recognition or dissappointment.

The girl, uneasily aware of Simmonds' attitude, moved on. Simmonds lingered for the last pull at his flask, and tossed it empty, over the cliff.

"There's no hurry," he said, as he caught up with her. "Lots of time—to enjoy things."

His speech had thickened, and Nora Manners noticed it as she caught the sickening odor of the liquor on his breath and the plainly impudent leer in his eyes as he blocked the trail.

"How dare you!" she gasped, stepping backward.

"Hol' on, sweetie," said Simmonds. "You'll slip and break your precious neck. Much too precious, worth lotsh."

He put out a hand and she struck it aside. She was frightened, but not panic-stricken.

"Stand out of my way!" she ordered.

Simmonds laughed.

"Hit me, will you?" he said, not pleasantly. "I'll make you pay for that," he added with a sudden savagery. He closed in on her, and she struck at him with her alpenstock. He tore it from her and flung it away, trying to take her in his arms, his whisky-laden breath coming thickly, his eyes suffused with blood.

She struggled fiercely as his clutch bruised her flesh and his bestial face neared hers.

"Pay for it—and plenty, d'ye hear?" he panted.

Gradually he forced her backwards, one rough arm about her, compelling her to his coarse embrace, his right hand vising her left wrist, bruising the flesh. She saw his eyes changing to madness, the light of manhood eclipsed by the glare of the brute. Struggling furiously, she stumbled, felt the strength running out of her and, with a desperate wrench, tore her wrist free and struck at the inflamed and leering features with all her strength. The stone in her ring slashed the flesh above his eye and the blood spurted, trickled scalding between his eyelids, while she hit him again, pounding now with both hands. Half blinded, furious, he tried to trip her, to fling her down.

Stark ugly fear possessed her!

"Damn you!" he panted, thickly. "I'll teach you a lesson. I'll——"

He tried to clear the blood from his eyes with the back of his hand and in that moment she twisted clear and fled wildly up the path. For a little she held her lead, but fright had overtaxed her while, behind her, she knew that the man had flung aside all restraints, was nothing but a ravening beast.

A loose stone slid and turned underfoot; her ankle twisted, and she fell on the narrow trail with Simmonds only a stride behind.

"Gotcha!" he cried with a hoarse chuckle.

The girl on one knee looked wildly about her. She seemed to lack all vigor. About was the rough, lonely mountainside, the harsh, windbitten trees, the hard, blue sky.

"*God!* Help me!" she did not know that the prayer had passed her lips until she heard the taunting laugh of Simmonds, bending over her.

Then, on the ledge above her, there appeared a gaunt, gray-brindle form. It looked like a gigantic timber wolf.

To the girl, with the mountainside seeming to rise and fall about her like a sea, it seemed for a mad moment as a phantom, an apparition conjured from her brain in the hideous, helpless situation. She had called on God. This thing might be the Spirit of Evil summoned by the man who no longer stooped over her but had straightened, his hand splayed wide, seeking the gun he no longer carried, since they were forbidden in the Park, seeking a knife he lacked, grizzly fear crawling upon his skin as he noted the swing of the gray head toward him, the lift of lips, the gleam of teeth and heard the low thunder of a guttural growl.

The girl's sight blurred, then cleared. Thus, surely, was an answer to her prayer. Here was no wolf. It was—it must be—Boru!

She called to him.

．　　．　　．　　．　　．　　．　　．　　．

It was a dramatic moment for Boru. Once again, as when he had turned back to rescue his mate from the fire, he was beset, shocked with varying emotions. Through scent and sight, to his vibrant nerve centers and so quivering through to his motor ganglia, there sped the emotions of love and of hate. For a few heartbeats he stood bewildered, short-circuited with conflicting sensations, urges, that nullified one the other.

Here was the being with whom he had associated all that was gentle and kind. The being whom he reverenced with a love beyond all selfishness. There was that within him, Nature planted, that demanded someone to worship, and to her he had long ago given love. Through brooding days and nights old memories had awakened, and now they came clamoring like a sudden thirst that could only be quenched by the touch of her hand, the sound of her voice.

Sight told him this, as it told him of the presence of the man who had tortured him, who had once been within the clip of his jaws.

But the savor of the girl, that should have been as fragrance to his eager nostrils, was tainted with fear, even as a flower, sweet in its blossoming, nauseates in decay. Fear came up the hill, flowing on a current of air. Fear from her he loved, and a blend of fear that slowly mastered hate, from the man.

So he stood at gaze, webbed in a complex of sense and emotion. Her voice broke the spell, lifted in desperate appeal—to him.

"Boru—*Boru!*"

For a pounding heartbeat she told herself that she had been mistaken. Then she caught a gleam in the dog's eyes, an old, familiar, quick lift of his muzzle, a swing of his tail before it stiffened as he crouched to a leap, his eyes charged with inplacable will to kill that flamed through all his great body and gave it a catapulting impetus. A hundred and a quarter pounds of bone and muscle and hard flesh sprang down the trail, clearing his mistress in a soaring leap, his great paws thrust to strike down his enemy, his jaws slavering to rend.

Courage left Simmonds as water leaves a vessel whose bottom has broken out. He saw two blazing eyes, fangs asnarl, a hurtling shape, and he flung up his arms with a wild yell of panic, instinctively jumping to one side, to go crashing through the scrub-oak thicket, anywhere to escape the ravening brute, to find a tree he could swing up into, a pile of rocks that he could scale and the dog could not.

"Hell! What devil brought that dog to arrive at such a moment?" To Simmonds, also, the dog seemed an evil conjuration as the question flared in his drink-muddled brain.

He did not know, any more than the girl, that here was no miracle, no fanciful coincidence, but the fair reward of Boru's patient hunting along the trail of love.

Simmonds was a thought too late. One great paw struck his shoulder, almost flung him down, sent him lurching through the brush, off balance, bent double, pitching to a fall, while Boru, landing, twisting his great body, wheeled to follow.

Simmonds had no sight, no sense of direction in that staggering, crashing lunge that he knew must end in a tumble. He should have known—he had known vaguely—that the mountain's side was cleft as if a mammoth ax had cloven it in back ages. An earthquake may have created the fissure, certainly it had later been filled with ice, ground by it until it was almost mirror smooth, a sheer slide of granite on which nothing grew. A hundred feet from its lip there was a slight jut, a few inches wide, of diamond-hard purple porphyry and then again the cliff became a vertical wall to the bottom of the great wedge which was choked by undergrowth and trees that had grown in the decomposing detritus accumulated there.

Still blundering, off balance from the thrust of Boru's paw, with the weight of his body back of it, Simmonds sprawled headlong just where the scrub oaks ceased abruptly. His arms, his head and shoulders slid out beyond the edge and, for one awful second, he gazed into the gulf while he frantically thrashed to hook a leg about the brush, to dig his toes into the shallow dirt—and failed. He shot into the cleft, braked a little by his efforts, falling head first. His hands hit the porphyry ledge, slid over its weather-polished glaze, his head struck it, pulped like a broken pumpkin, and then his limp body somersaulted and went whirling down. . . .

At that instant Boru arrived in a great leap on the cliff's margin, plowing to a halt. He had his four legs, armed with separate pads and stout claws, to aid him. He braced them rigid and halted, gazing down to where something limp and heavy crashed through the branches two hundred feet below.

He whined, puzzled. His enemy had escaped him. He started to bark and then the quick prescience of death came to him. He flung back his head and howled—howled with a note of triumph in the weird ululation.

One hand against her pounding heart, the girl peered through the brush and saw him standing there—alone. Simmonds' hat was at her feet where the scrub growth had clawed it off. She looked down at a splintered branch far below. Then she made out something crumpled up among the top boughs, like an entangled kite, a thing of cloth, and flesh, and broken bone.

She came back to consciousness with Boru nuzzling her face. Revulsion still held her faint but strength was coming back. She sat up with her arms about the dog's sturdy neck, glad of its hard vigor, burying her face in the rough hair.

Boru stood still as a statue, save for the outrun of his tongue and the glad beat of his tail.   He was content.   His Odyssey was ended.   He had come home!

There's More to Follow!

More stories of the sort you like; more, probably, by the author of this one; more than 500 titles all told by writers of world-wide reputation, in the Authors' Alphabetical List which you will find on the *reverse side* of the wrapper of this book. Look it over before you lay it aside. There are books here you are sure to want—some, possibly, that you have *always* wanted.

It is a *selected* list; every book in it has achieved a certain measure of *success.*

The Grosset & Dunlap list is not only the greatest Index of Good Fiction available, it represents in addition a generally accepted Standard of Value. It will pay you to

Look on the Other Side of the Wrapper!

In case the wrapper is lost write to the publishers for a complete catalog

JACK LONDON'S NOVELS

Tales of strong hearts, men and women, in the frozen wastes of the Land of Eternal Snows, tales of splendid courage and adventure on the sailing ships of the seven seas, tales of the blacks and the whites of the Far-away Islands, and tales of wanderings and roamings in many lands.

BURNING DAYLIGHT

CALL OF THE WILD, THE

DAUGHTER OF THE SNOWS, A

JERRY, OF THE ISLANDS

MICHAEL, BROTHER OF JERRY

SEA WOLF, THE

SMOKE BELLEW

SON OF THE WOLF, THE

VALLEY OF THE MOON, THE

WHITE FANG

GROSSET & DUNLAP, *Publishers*, NEW YORK

NOVELS OF FRONTIER LIFE
WILLIAM Mac LEOD RAINE

May be had wherever books are sold.   Ask for Grosset and Dunlap's list.

GROSSET & DUNLAP, *Publishers,*   NEW YORK

ZANE GREY'S NOVELS

May be had wherever books are sold. Ask for Grosset and Dunlap's list.

UNDER THE TONTO RIM
TAPPAN'S BURRO
THE VANISHING AMERICAN
THE THUNDERING HERD
THE CALL OF THE CANYON
WANDERER OF THE WASTELAND
TO THE LAST MAN
THE MYSTERIOUS RIDER
THE MAN OF THE FOREST
THE DESERT OF WHEAT
THE U. P. TRAIL
WILDFIRE
THE BORDER LEGION
THE RAINBOW TRAIL
THE HERITAGE OF THE DESERT
RIDERS OF THE PURPLE SAGE
THE LIGHT OF WESTERN STARS
THE LAST OF THE PLAINSMEN
THE LONE STAR RANGER
DESERT GOLD
BETTY ZANE
THE DAY OF THE BEAST

* * * * * * *

LAST OF THE GREAT SCOUTS
  The life story of "Buffalo Bill" by his sister Helen Cody
Wetmore, with Foreword and conclusion by Zane Grey.

ZANE GREY'S BOOKS FOR BOYS

ROPING LIONS IN THE GRAND CANYON
KEN WARD IN THE JUNGLE
THE YOUNG LION HUNTER
THE YOUNG FORESTER
THE YOUNG PITCHER
THE SHORT STOP
THE RED-HEADED OUTFIELD AND OTHER
  BASEBALL STORIES

GROSSET & DUNLAP, *Publishers,* NEW YORK

JAMES OLIVER CURWOOD'S
STORIES OF ADVENTURE

THE ANCIENT HIGHWAY

A GENTLEMAN OF COURAGE

THE ALASKAN

THE COUNTRY BEYOND

THE FLAMING FOREST

THE VALLEY OF SILENT MEN

THE RIVER'S END

THE GOLDEN SNARE

NOMADS OF THE NORTH

KAZAN

BAREE, SON OF KAZAN

THE COURAGE OF CAPTAIN PLUM

THE DANGER TRAIL

THE HUNTED WOMAN

THE FLOWER OF THE NORTH

THE GRIZZLY KING

ISOBEL

THE WOLF HUNTERS

THE GOLD HUNTERS

THE COURAGE OF MARGE O'DOONE

BACK TO GOD'S COUNTRY

GROSSET & DUNLAP, *Publishers,* NEW YORK

B. M. BOWER'S NOVELS

BLACK THUNDER

HERITAGE OF THE SIOUX

MEADOWLARK BASIN

DESERT BREW

BELLEHELEN MINE, THE

EAGLE'S WING, THE

PAROWAN BONANZA, THE

VOICE AT JOHNNYWATER, THE

CASEY RYAN

CHIP OF THE FLYING U

FLYING U RANCH

FLYING U'S LAST STAND, THE

HAPPY FAMILY, THE

HER PRAIRIE KNIGHT

LONG SHADOW, THE

LONESOME TRAIL, THE

LOOKOUT MAN, THE

LURE OF THE DIM TRAILS, THE

PHANTOM HERD, THE

RANGE DWELLERS, THE

RIM O' THE WORLD

STARR OF THE DESERT

TRAIL OF THE WHITE MULE, THE

UPHILL CLIMB, THE

GROSSET & DUNLAP, PUBLISHERS, NEW YORK